"I had no idea that you had it in you,"

Sir Colin told Eustacia, after their company had gone.

"Had what, Sir Colin?"

"This ability to be a loving fiancée at a moment's notice, although I could have wished for a few more melting glances."

"Well, I didn't want to overdo it."

"That would be impossible." He took her arm and walked her into the house. "Now, when shall we get married?"

She turned to face him. "You aren't serious?" She studied his face and decided that he was.

"Am I to be jilted before we are even officially engaged? I had thought better of you, Eustacia."

Betty Neels is well-known for her romances set in the Netherlands, which is hardly surprising. She married a Dutchman and spent the first twelve years of their marriage living in Holland and working as a nurse. Today, she and her husband make their home in an ancient stone cottage in England's West Country, but they return to Holland often. She loves to explore tiny villages and tour privately owned homes there, in order to lend an air of authenticity to the background of her books.

Books by Betty Neels

Don't miss any of our special offers. Write to us at the following address for information on our newest releases.

Harlequin Reader Service
P.O. Box 1397, Buffalo, NY 14240
Canadian address: P.O. Box 603,
Fort Erie, Ont. L2A 5X3

A SUITABLE MATCH

Betty Neels

Harlequin Books

TORONTO • NEW YORK • LONDON
AMSTERDAM • PARIS • SYDNEY • HAMBURG
STOCKHOLM • ATHENS • TOKYO • MILAN

Original hardcover edition published in 1990
by Mills & Boon Limited

ISBN 0-373-03131-9

Harlequin Romance first edition June 1991

A SUITABLE MATCH

CHAPTER ONE

EUSTACIA bit into her toast, poured herself another cup of tea, and turned her attention once again to the job vacancies in the morning paper. She had been doing this for some days now and it was with no great hope of success that she ran her eye down the columns. Her qualifications, which were few, didn't seem to fit into any of the jobs on offer. It was a pity, she reflected, that an education at a prestigious girls' school had left her quite unfitted for earning her living in the commercial world. She had done her best, but the course of shorthand and typing had been nothing less than disastrous, and she hadn't lasted long at the boutique because, unlike her colleagues, she had found herself quite incapable of telling a customer that a dress fitted while she held handfuls of surplus material at that lady's back, or left a zip undone to accommodate surplus flesh. She had applied for a job at the local post office too, and had been turned down because she didn't wish to join a union. No one, it seemed, wanted a girl with four A levels and the potential for a university if she had been able to go to one. Here she was, twenty-two years old, out of work once more and with a grandfather to support.

She bent her dark head over the pages—she was a pretty girl with eyes as dark as her hair, a dainty little nose and a rather too large mouth—eating her toast absentmindedly as she searched the pages. There was nothing... Yes, there was: the path lab of St Biddolph's Hospital, not half a mile away, needed an assistant bottle-washer, general cleaner and postal worker. No qualifications required other than honesty, speed and cleanliness. The pay wasn't bad either.

Eustacia swallowed the rest of her tea, tore out the advertisement, and went out of the shabby little room into the passage and tapped on a door. A voice told her to go in and she did so, a tall, splendidly built girl wearing what had once been a good suit, now out of date but immaculate.

'Grandpa,' she began, addressing the old man sitting up in his bed. 'There's a job in this morning's paper. As soon as I've brought your breakfast I'm going after it.'

The old gentleman looked at her over his glasses. 'What kind of a job?'

'Assistant at the path lab at St Biddolph's.' She beamed at him. 'It sounds OK, doesn't it?' She whisked herself through the door again. 'I'll be back in five minutes with your tray.'

She left their small ground-floor flat in one of the quieter streets of Kennington and walked briskly to the bus-stop. It wasn't yet nine o'clock and speed, she felt, was of the essence. Others, it seemed, had felt the same; there were six women already in the little waiting-room inside the entrance to the path lab at the hospital, and within the next ten minutes another four turned up. Eustacia sat there quietly waiting, uttering silent, childish prayers. This job would be nothing less than a godsend—regular hours, fifteen minutes from the flat and the weekly pay-packet would be enough to augment her grandfather's pension—a vital point, this, for they had been eating into their tiny capital for several weeks.

Her turn came and she went to the room set aside for the interviews, and sat down before a stout, elderly man sitting at a desk. He looked bad-tempered and he sounded it too, ignoring her polite 'Good morning' and plunging at once into his own questions.

She answered them briefly, handed over her references and waited for him to speak.

"You have four A levels. Why are you not at a university?'

'Family circumstances,' said Eustacia matter-of-factly.

He glanced up. 'Yes, well . . . the work here is menial, you understand that?' He glowered across the desk at her. 'You will be notified.'

Not very hopeful, she considered, walking back to the flat; obviously A levels weren't of much help when applying for such a job. She would give it a day and, if she heard nothing, she would try for something else. She stopped at the baker's and bought bread and then went next door to the greengrocer's and chose a cauliflower. Cauliflower cheese for supper and some carrots and potatoes. She had become adept at making soup now that October was sliding into November. At least she could cook, an art she had been taught at her expensive boarding-school, and if it hadn't been for her grandfather she might have tried her luck as a cook in some hotel. Indeed, she had left school with no thought of training for anything; her mother and father had been alive then, full of ideas about taking her with them when they travelled. 'Plenty of time,' they had said. 'A couple of years enjoying life before you marry or decide what you want to do,' and she had had those two years, seeing quite a lot of the world, knowing only vaguely that her father was in some kind of big business which allowed them to live in comfort. It was when he and her mother had been killed in an air crash that she'd discovered that he was heavily in debt, that his business was bankrupt and that any money there was would have to go to creditors. It had been frightening to find herself without a penny and an urgent necessity to earn a living, and it had been then that her grandfather, someone she had seldom met for he'd lived in the north of England, had come to see her.

'We have each other,' he had told her kindly. 'I cannot offer you a home, for my money was invested in your father's business, but I have my pension and I believe I know someone who will help us to find something modest to live in in London.'

He had been as good as his word; the 'someone' owned property in various parts of London and they had moved into the flat two years ago, and Eustacia had set about getting a job. Things hadn't been too bad at first, but her typing and shorthand weren't good enough to get a job in a office and her grandfather had developed a heart condition so that she had had to stay at home for some time to look after him. Now, she thought hopefully, perhaps their luck had changed and she would get this job, and Grandfather would get better, well enough for her to hire a car and take him to Kew or Richmond Park. He hated the little street where they lived and longed for the country, and so secretly did she, although she never complained. He had enough to bear, she considered, and felt nothing but gratitude for his kindness when she had needed it most.

She made coffee for them both when she got in and told him about the job. 'There were an awful lot of girls there,' she said. 'This man said he would let me know. I don't expect that means much, but it's better than being told that the job's been taken—I mean, I can go on hoping until I hear.'

She heard two days later—the letter was on the mat when she got up, and she took it to the kitchen and put on the kettle for their morning tea and opened it.

The job was hers—she was to present herself for work on the following Monday at eight-thirty sharp. She would have half an hour for her lunch, fifteen minutes for her coffee-break and tea in the afternoon, and work until five o'clock. She would be free on Saturdays and Sundays but once a month she would be required to work on Saturday, when she would be allowed the following Monday free. Her wages, compared to Grandfather's pension, seemed like a fortune.

She took a cup of tea to her grandfather and told him the news.

'I'm glad, my dear. It will certainly make life much easier for you—now you will be able to buy yourself some pretty clothes.'

It wasn't much good telling him that pretty clothes weren't any use unless she had somewhere to go in them, but she agreed cheerfully, while she did sums in her head: the gas bill, always a formidable problem with her grandfather to keep warm by the gas fire in their sitting-room—duvets for their beds, some new saucepans... She mustn't get too ambitious, she told herself cautiously, and went off to get herself dressed.

She got up earlier than usual on Monday, tidied the flat, saw to her grandfather's small wants, cautioned him to be careful while she was away, kissed him affectionately, and started off for the hospital.

She was a little early, but that didn't matter, as it gave her time to find her way around to the cubby-hole where she was to change into the overall she was to wear, and peep into rooms and discover where the canteen was. A number of people worked at the path lab and they could get a meal cheaply enough as well as coffee and tea. People began to arrive and presently she was told to report to an office on the ground floor where she was given a list of duties she was to do by a brisk lady who made no attempt to disguise her low opinion of Eustacia's job.

'You will wear rubber gloves at all times and a protective apron when you are emptying discarded specimens. I hope you are strong.'

Eustacia hoped she was, too.

By the end of the first day she concluded that a good deal of her work comprised washing-up—glass containers, dishes, little pots, glass tubes and slides. There was the emptying of buckets, too, the distribution of clean laundry and the collecting of used overalls for the porters to bag, and a good deal of toing and froing, taking sheaves of papers, specimens and the post to wherever it was wanted. She was tired as she went home; there were, she supposed, pleasanter ways of earning a living, but never mind that, she was already looking forward to her pay-packet at the end of the week.

She had been there for three days when she came face to face with the man who had interviewed her. He stopped in front of her and asked, 'Well, do you like your work?'

She decided that despite his cross face he wasn't ill-disposed towards her. 'I'm glad to have work,' she told him pleasantly, 'you have no idea how glad. Not all my work is—well, nice, but of course you know that already.'

He gave a rumble of laughter. 'No one stays for long,' he told her. 'Plenty of applicants when the job falls vacant, but they don't last ...'

'I have every intention of staying, provided my work is satisfactory.' She smiled at him and he laughed again.

'Do you know who I am?'

'No. I don't know anyone yet—only to say good morning and so on. I saw Miss Bennett when I came here—she told me what to do and so on—and I've really had no time to ask anyone.'

'I'm in charge of this department, young lady; the name's Professor Ladbroke. I'll see that you get a list of those working here.'

He nodded and walked away. Oh, dear, thought Eustacia, I should have called him 'sir' and not said all that.

She lived in a state of near panic for the rest of the week, wondering if she would get the sack, but pay-day came and there was nothing in her envelope but money. She breathed a sigh of relief and vowed to mind her Ps and Qs in future.

No one took much notice of her; she went in and out of rooms peopled by quiet, white-coated forms peering through microscopes or doing mysterious things with tweezers and pipettes. She suspected that they didn't even see her, and the greater part of her day was concerned with the cleansing of endless bowls and dishes. It was, she discovered, a lonely life, but towards the end of the second week one or two people wished her good morning and an austere man with a beard asked her if she found the work hard.

She told him no, adding cheerfully, 'A bit off-putting sometimes, though!' He looked surprised, and she wished that she hadn't said anything at all.

By the end of the third week she felt as though she had been there for years—she was even liking her work. There actually was a certain pleasure in keeping things clean and being useful, in however humble a capacity, to a department full of silent, dedicated people, all so hard at work with their microscopes and pipettes and little glass dishes.

She was to work that Saturday; she walked home, shopping on her way, buying food which her grand-father could see to on his own, thankful that she didn't have to look at every penny. In the morning she set out cheerfully for the hospital. There would be a skeleton staff in the path lab until midday, and after that she had been told to pass any urgent messages to whoever was on call that weekend. One of the porters would come on duty at six o'clock that evening and take over the phone when she went.

The department was quiet; she went around, changing linen, opening windows, making sure that there was a supply of tea and sugar and milk in the small kitchen, and then carefully filling the half-empty shelves with towels, soap, stationery and path lab forms and, lastly, making sure that there was enough of everything in the sterilisers. It took her until mid-morning, by which time the staff on duty had arrived and were busy dealing with whatever had been sent from the hospital. She made coffee for them all, had some herself and went to assemble fresh supplies of dishes and bowls on trays ready for sterilising. She was returning from carrying a load from one room to the next when she came face to face with a man.

She was a tall girl, but she had to look up to see his face. A handsome one it was too, with a commanding nose, drooping lids over blue eyes and a thin mouth. His hair was thick and fair and rather untidy, and he was wearing a long white coat—he was also very large.

He stopped in front of her. 'Ah, splendid, get this checked at once, will you, and let me have the result? I'll be in the main theatre. It's urgent.' He handed her a covered kidney dish. 'Do I know you?'

'No,' said Eustacia. She spoke to his broad, retreating back.

He had said it was urgent; she bore the dish to Mr Brimshaw, who was crouching over something nasty in a tray. He waved her away as she reached him, but she stood her ground.

'Someone—a large man in a white coat—gave me this and said he would be in the main theatre and that it was urgent.'

'Then don't stand there, girl, give it to me.'

As she went away he called after her. 'Come back in ten minutes, and you can take it back.'

'Such manners,' muttered Eustacia as she went back to her dishes.

In exactly ten minutes she went back again to Mr Brimshaw just in time to prevent him from opening his mouth to bellow for her. He gave a grunt instead. 'And look sharp about it,' he cautioned her.

The theatre block wasn't anywhere near the path lab; she nipped smartly in and out of lifts and along corridors and finally, since the lifts were already in use, up a flight of stairs. She hadn't been to the theatre block before and she wasn't sure how far inside the swing-doors she was allowed to go, a problem solved for her by the reappearance of the man in the white coat, only now he was in a green tunic and trousers and a green cap to match.

He took the kidney dish from her with a nice smile. 'Good girl—new, aren't you?' He turned to go and then paused. 'What is your name?'

'Eustacia Crump.' She flew back through the swing-doors, not wanting to hear him laugh—everyone laughed when she told them her name. Eustacia and Crump didn't go well together. He didn't laugh, only stood for a moment more watching her splendid person, swathed in its ill-fitting overall, disappear.

Mr Brimshaw went home at one o'clock and Jim Walker, one of the more senior pathologists working under him, took over. He was a friendly young man and, since Eustacia had done all that was required of her and there was nothing much for him to do for half an hour, she made him tea and had a cup herself with her sandwiches. She became immersed in a reference book of pathological goings-on—she understood very little of it, but it made interesting reading.

It fell to her to go to theatre again a couple of hours later, this time with a vacoliter of blood.

'Mind and bring back that form, properly signed,' warned Mr Walker. 'And don't loiter, will you? They're in a hurry.'

Eustacia went. Who, she asked herself, would wish to loiter in such circumstances? Did Mr Walker think that she would tuck the thing under one arm and stop for a chat with anyone she might meet on her way? She was terrified of dropping it anyway.

She sighed with relief when she reached the theatre block and went cautiously through the swing-doors, only to pause because she wasn't quite sure where to go. A moot point settled for her by a disapproving voice behind her.

'There you are,' said a cross-faced nurse, and took the vacoliter from her.

Eustacia waved the form at her. 'This has to be signed, please.'

'Well, of course it does.' It was taken from her and the nurse plunged through one of the doors on either side, just as the theatre door at the far end swished open and the tall man she had met in the path lab came through.

'Brought the blood?' he asked pleasantly, and when she nodded, 'Miss Crump, isn't it? We met recently.' He stood in front of her, apparently in no haste.

'Tell me,' he asked, 'why are you not sitting on a bench doing blood counts and looking at cells instead of washing bottles?'

It was a serious question and it deserved a serious answer.

'Well, that's what I am—a bottle-washer, although it's called a path lab assistant, and I'm not sure that I should like to sit at a bench all day—some of the things that are examined are very nasty...'

His eyes crinkled nicely at the corners when he smiled. 'They are. You don't look like a bottle-washer.'

'Oh? Do they look different from anyone else?'

He didn't answer that but went on. 'You are far too beautiful,' he told her, and watched her go a delicate pink.

A door opened and the cross nurse came back with the form in her hand. When she saw them she smoothed the ill humour from her face and smiled.

'I've been looking everywhere for you, sir. If you would sign this form...?' She cast Eustacia a look of great superiority as she spoke. 'They're waiting in theatre for you, sir,' she added in what Eustacia considered to be an oily voice.

The man took the pen she offered and scrawled on the paper and handed it to Eustacia. 'Many thanks, Miss Crump,' he said with grave politeness. He didn't look at the nurse once but went back through the theatre door without a backward glance.

The nurse tossed her head at Eustacia. 'Well, hadn't you better get back to the path lab?' she wanted to know. 'You've wasted enough of our time already.'

Eustacia was almost a head taller, and it gave her a nice feeling of superiority. 'Rubbish,' she said crisply, 'and shouldn't you be doing whatever you ought instead of standing there?'

She didn't stay to hear what the other girl had to say; she hoped that she wouldn't be reported for rudeness.

It had been silly of her to annoy the nurse; she couldn't afford to jeopardise her job.

'OK?' asked Mr Walker when she gave him back the signed form. He glanced at it. 'Ah, signed by the great man himself...'

'Oh, a big man in his theatre kit? I don't know anyone here.'

Mr Walker said rather unkindly, 'Well, you don't need to, do you? He's Sir Colin Crichton. An honorary consultant here—goes all over the place—he's specialising in cancer treatment—gets good results too.' He looked at his watch. 'Make me some tea, will you? There's a good girl.'

She put on the kettle and waited while it boiled and thought about Sir Colin Crichton. He had called her Miss Crump and he hadn't laughed. She liked him, and she wished she could see him again.

However, she didn't, the week passed and Saturday came again and she was free once more. Because it was a beautiful day—a bonus at the beginning of the winter—she helped her grandfather to wrap up warmly, went out and found a taxi, and took him to Kew Gardens. Supported by her arm and a stick, the old gentleman walked its paths, inspected a part of the botanical gardens, listened to the birds doing their best in the pale sunshine and then expressed a wish to go to the Orangery.

It was there that they encountered Sir Colin, accompanied by two small boys. Eustacia saw him first and suggested hastily to her grandfather that they might turn around and stroll in the opposite direction.

'Why ever should we do that?' he asked testily, and before she could think up a good reason Sir Colin had reached them.

'Ah—Miss Crump. We share a similar taste in Chambers' work—a delightful spot on a winter morning.'

He stood looking at her, his eyebrows faintly lifted, and after a moment she said, 'Good morning, sir,' and, since her grandfather was looking at her as well, 'Grandfather, this is Sir Colin Crichton, he's a consultant at St Biddolph's. My Grandfather, Mr Henry Crump.'

The two men shook hands and the boys were introduced—Teddy and Oliver, who shook hands too, and, since the two gentlemen had fallen into conversation and had fallen into step, to stroll the length of the Orangery and then back into the gardens again, Eustacia found herself with the two boys. They weren't very old—nine years, said Teddy, and Oliver was a year younger. They were disposed to like her and within a few minutes were confiding a number of interesting facts. Half-term, they told her, and they would go back to school on Monday, and had she any brothers who went away to school?

She had to admit that she hadn't. 'But I really am very interested; do tell me what you do there—I don't mean lessons...'

They understood her very well. She was treated to a rigmarole of Christmas plays, football, computer games and what a really horrible man the maths master was. 'Well, I dare say your father can help you with your homework,' she suggested.

'Oh, he's much too busy,' said Oliver, and she supposed that he was, operating and doing ward rounds and out-patients and travelling around besides. He couldn't have much home life. She glanced back to where the two men were strolling at her grandfather's pace along the path towards them, deep in talk. She wondered if Sir Colin wanted to take his leave but was too courteous to say so; his wife might be waiting at home for him and the boys. She spent a few moments deciding what to do and rather reluctantly turned back towards them.

'We should be getting back,' she suggested to her grandfather, and was echoed at once by Sir Colin.

'So must we. Allow me to give you a lift—the car's by the Kew Road entrance.'

Before her grandfather could speak, Eustacia said quickly, 'That's very kind of you, but I daresay we live in a quite opposite direction to you: Kennington.'

'It couldn't be more convenient,' she was told smoothly. 'We can keep south of the river, drop you off and cross at Southwark.' He gave her a gentle smile and at the same time she saw that he intended to have his own way.

They walked to the main gate, suiting their pace to that of her grandfather, and got into the dark blue Rolls-Royce parked there. Eustacia sat between the boys at the back, surprised to find that they were sharing it with a small, untidy dog with an extremely long tail and melting brown eyes. Moreover, he had a leg in plaster.

'This is Moses,' said Oliver as he squashed in beside Eustacia. 'He was in the water with a broken leg,' he explained and, since Eustacia looked so astonished, said it for a second time, rather loudly, just as though she were deaf.

'Oh, the poor little beast.' She bent to rub the unruly head at their feet and Sir Colin, settling himself in the driving-seat, said over his shoulder, 'He's not quite up to walking far, but he likes to be with us. Unique, isn't he?'

'But nice,' said Eustacia, and wished she could think of a better word.

It was quite a lengthy drive; she sat between the boys, taking part in an animated conversation on such subjects as horrendous schoolmasters, their favourite TV programmes, their dislike of maths and their favourite food. She found them both endearing and felt regret when the drive was over and the car drew up before their flat. Rolls-Royces were a rarity in the neighbourhood, and it would be a talking-point for some time—already curtains in neighbouring houses were being twitched.

She wished the boys goodbye and they chorused an urgent invitation to go out with them again, and, conscious of Sir Colin's hooded eyes upon her, she murmured non-committally, bending to stroke Moses because she could feel herself blushing hatefully.

She waited while her grandfather expressed his thanks for the ride, and then she added her own thanks with a frank look from her dark eyes, to encounter his smiling gaze.

'We have enjoyed your company,' he told her, and she found herself believing him. 'The boys get bored, you know; I haven't all that time at home and my housekeeper is elderly and simply can't cope with them.'

'Housekeeper? Oh, I thought they were yours.'

'My brother's. He has gone abroad with his wife, a job in Brunei for a few months. They are too young for boarding-school...'

They had shaken hands and he still held hers in a firm grasp.

'They like you,' he said.

'Well, I like them. I'm glad I met them and Grandfather has enjoyed himself. He doesn't get out much.'

He nodded and gave her back her hand and went to open the rickety gate, and waited while they went up the short path to the front door and opened it. Eustacia turned as they went inside and smiled at them all, before he closed the gate, got back into his car and drove away.

'A delightful morning, my dear,' said her grandfather. 'I feel ten years younger—and such an interesting conversation. You are most fortunate to be working for such a man.'

'Well, I don't,' said Eustacia matter-of-factly. 'I only met him because he came down to the path lab for something. He goes to St Biddolph's once or twice a week to operate and see his patients, and as I seldom leave the path lab except when there is a message to run we don't meet.'

'Yes, yes,' her grandfather sounded testy, 'but now that you have met you will see more of each other.'

She thought it best not to argue further; she suspected that he had no idea of the work she did. Sir Colin had been charming but that didn't mean to say that he wished to pursue their acquaintance; indeed it was most unlikely. A pity, she reflected as she went to the kitchen to get their lunch, but they occupied different worlds—she would probably end up by marrying another bottle-washer. A sobering thought even while she laughed at the idea.

It was December in no time at all, or so it seemed, and the weather turned cold and damp and dark, and the shops began to fill with Christmas food and a splendid array of suitable presents. Eustacia did arithmetic on the backs of envelopes, made lists and began to hoard things like chocolate biscuits, strawberry jam, tins of ham and a Christmas pudding; she had little money over each week and she laid it out carefully, determined to have a good Christmas. There would be no one to visit, of course. As far as she knew they had no family, and her grandfather's friends lived in the north of England and her own friends from school days were either married or holding down good jobs with no time to spare. From time to time they exchanged letters, but pride prevented her from telling any of them about the change in her life. She wrote cheerful replies, telling them nothing in a wealth of words.

On the first Saturday in December it was her lot to work all day. Mr Brimshaw arrived some time after she did, wished her a grumpy good morning and went into his own office, and she began on her chores. It was a dismal day and raining steadily, but she busied herself with her dishes and pots, made coffee for Mr Brimshaw and herself and thought about Christmas. She would have liked a new dress but that was out of the question—she had spent more than she could afford on a thick waistcoat for her grandfather and a pair of woollen gloves, and there was still something to be bought for their landlady, who, although kindly disposed towards them as long as the rent was paid on time, needed to be kept sweet. A headscarf, mused Eustacia, or perhaps a box of soap? She was so deep in thought that Mr Brimshaw had to bawl twice before she heard him.

'Hurry up, girl—Casualty's full—there's been an accident in Oxford Street and they'll be shouting for blood before I can take a breath. Get along with this first batch and then come back as fast as you can.'

He had cross-matched another victim when she got back, so she hurried away for a second time with another vacoliter and after that she lost count of the times she trotted to and fro. The initial urgency settled down presently and Mr Brimshaw, crosser than ever because he was late for his lunch, went home and Mr Walker took over, and after that things became a little more settled. All the same, she was tired when the evening porter came on duty and she was able to go home. It was still raining; she swathed her person in her elderly raincoat, tied a scarf over her hair and made for the side entrance. It being Saturday, there wouldn't be all that number of buses which meant that they would be full too. She nipped smartly across the courtyard, head down against the rain, and went full tilt into Sir Colin, coming the other way. He took her considerable weight without any effort and stood her on to her feet.

'Going home?' he wanted to know gently.

She nodded and then said, 'Oh...' when he took her arm and turned her round.

'So am I. I'll drop you off on my way.'

'But I'm wet, I'll spoil your car.'

'Don't be silly,' he begged her nicely. 'I'm wet too.'

He bustled her to the car and settled her into the front seat and got in beside her.

'It's out of your way,' sighed Eustacia weakly.

'Not at all—what a girl you are for finding objections.'

They sat in a comfortable silence as he turned the car in the direction of the river and Kennington. That he had only just arrived at the hospital intent on having a few words with his registrar, when he saw her, was something he had no intention of revealing. He wasn't at all sure why he had offered to take her home; he hardly knew her and although he found her extremely pretty and, what was more, intelligent, he had made no conscious effort to seek her out. It was a strange fact that two people could meet and feel instantly at ease with each other—more than that, feel as though they had known each other all their lives. Eustacia, sitting quietly beside him, was thinking exactly the same thing.

He smiled nicely when she thanked him, got out of the car and opened the gate for her and waited until she had unlocked the door and gone inside before driving himself back to the hospital, thinking about her. She was too good for the job she was doing, and like a beautiful fish out of water in that depressing little street.

He arrived back at St Biddolph's and became immersed in the care of his patients, shutting her delightful image away in the back of his mind and keeping it firmly there.

CHAPTER TWO

THE path lab would be open over Christmas; accidents and sudden illness took no account of holidays. Eustacia was to work on Christmas Day morning and again on Boxing Day afternoon, sharing the days with the two porters. She went home on Christmas Eve much cheered by the good wishes and glass of sherry she had been offered before everyone left that evening. Once there, she opened the bottle of claret she had been hoarding and she and her grandfather toasted each other before they sat down to supper. She had bought a chicken for their Christmas dinner, and before she went to bed she prepared everything for the meal so that when she got back home the next day she would need only to put the food in the oven. In the morning she got up earlier than usual, laid the table and put the presents they had for each other beside the small Christmas tree, took her grandfather his breakfast and then hurried off to work. There was no one there save the night porter, who wished her a hasty 'Merry Christmas' before hurrying off duty. He hadn't had to call anyone up during the night, he told her, and hoped that she would have a quiet morning.

Which indeed she did. Mr Brimshaw, arriving shortly afterwards, wished her a mumbled 'Happy Christmas' and went along to his office to deal with the paperwork, and Eustacia set about putting the place to rights, turning out cupboards and then making coffee. The telephone went incessantly but there were no emergencies; at one o'clock the second porter took over and Mr Brimshaw handed over to one of the assistants. Eustacia went to

23

get her outdoor things, wished the porter a civil goodbye and made for the door just as one of the hospital porters came in with a parcel.

'Miss Crump?' he enquired. 'I was to deliver this before you left.'

'Me?' Eustacia beamed at him. 'You're sure it's for me?'

'Name's Crump, isn't it?'

He went away again and she tucked the gaily packed box under her arm and went home, speculating all the way as to who it was from.

But first when she got home there was her present from her grandfather to open—warm red slippers; just what she needed, she declared, during the cold months of winter. After he had admired his waistcoat and gloves she opened her package. It had been wrapped in red paper covered with robins and tied with red ribbons, and she gave a great sigh of pleasure when she saw its contents: an extravagantly large box of handmade chocolates, festooned with yet more ribbons and covered in brocade. There was a card with it, written in a childish hand, 'With Love from Oliver and Teddy.'

'Well, really,' said Eustacia, totally surprised. 'But I only met them once, remember, Grandfather, at Kew...'

'Children like to give presents to the people they like.'

'I must write and thank them—only I don't know where they live.'

'They're with their uncle, aren't they? And with luck someone at the hospital will surely know his address.'

'Yes, of course. What a lovely surprise. Have one while I start the dinner.' She paused on her way to the kitchen. 'It must have cost an awful lot, and they're only children.'

'I dare say they've been saving up—you know what children are.' Her grandfather chose a chocolate with care and popped it into his mouth. 'They're delicious.'

They had their dinner presently and afterwards Eustacia went to church, and went back home to watch television until bedtime. Without saying anything to her grandfather she had hired a set, to his great delight, for he spent a good part of the day on his own and she guessed that he was sometimes lonely. If, later on, she couldn't afford it, she could always return it—although, seeing the old man's pleasure in it, she vowed to keep it at all costs. It was an extravagance, she supposed, and the money should perhaps be saved against a rainy day or the ever-worrying chance that she might lose her job. On the other hand, it was their one extravagance and did much to lighten their uneventful lives.

She went back to work the next day after their lunch. There were two of the staff on duty, cross-matching blood for patients due for operations the following day, doing blood counts and checking test meals. Eustacia made tea for them both, had a cup herself and busied herself restocking the various forms on each bench. That done, she put out clean towels, filled the soap containers and cleaned the sinks which had been used. She was to stay until six o'clock when the night porter would take over, and once the others had gone it was very quiet. She was glad when he came to spend a few minutes in cheerful talk before she took herself off home.

Everyone was short-tempered in the morning—too much to eat and drink, too little sleep and a generally jaundiced outlook on life cast gloom over the entire department. Miss Bennett found fault with very nearly everything, until Eustacia felt like flinging a tray of dishes and bottles on to the floor and walking out for good. She held her tongue and looked meek, and to her great surprise at the day's end Miss Bennett rather grudgingly admitted that on the whole her work was quite satisfactory, adding sternly that there was to be no more slackness now that the festive season was over. 'And a good thing it is,' she observed. It was obvious to Eustacia that the poor woman found no joy in her life. Such a pity, one never knew what was round the corner.

It was halfway through January when she got home one evening to find, to her great astonishment, Sir Colin Crichton sitting all at ease opposite her grandfather's armchair by the open fire. He got up when she went in and wished her a polite good evening, and she replied with a hint of tartness. She wasn't looking at her best; it had been a busy day and she was tired, and, conscious that her hair was untidy and her face badly needed fresh make-up, the frown she turned upon him was really quite fierce and he smiled faintly.

'I came to talk to you,' he said to surprise her, 'but if you are too tired...?'

She took up the challenge. 'I am not in the least tired,' she assured him, and then said suddenly, 'Oh—is it about my job?'

He had sat down again and she glanced at her grandfather, who, beyond smiling at her when she kissed him, had remained silent.

'Er—yes, to a certain extent.'

She took an indignant breath. She had worked hard at a job she really didn't like and now she supposed she was to get the sack, although why someone as exalted as Sir Colin had to do it was beyond her.

He said in his quiet, deliberate voice, 'No, it is not what you think it is, Miss Crump, but it would please me very much if you would give up your job in the path lab and come to work for me.'

'Come to work for you?' she echoed his words in a voice squeaky with surprise. And then added, 'Why?'

'My nephews,' he explained. 'They have both had flu, tonsillitis and nasty chests. It is obvious that London doesn't agree with them, at least until they are fit again. I feel responsible for them while their mother and father are away, but I am rarely at home during the day and there is no question of their going back to school for several weeks. I have a home at Turville, just north of Henley. A very small village and quiet—I don't go there as often as I would wish. I should like the boys to go there and I would be glad if you would go with them. They have taken to you in a big way, you know.' He smiled his charming smile. 'There is a housekeeper there, her husband does the garden and the odd jobs but they are both elderly and the boys need young company—a kind of elder sister? I think that you would fill that role exactly...'

Eustacia had her mouth open to speak and he went on calmly, 'No, don't interrupt—let me finish... I am not sure how long it might be before my brother returns—but at least two months, and at the end of that time you would have sufficient experience to get a post in a similar capacity. There is plenty of room for everyone; the Samwayses have their own quarters on the ground floor at the back of the house and adjoining it is a bedroom which Mr Crump could use. You yourself, Miss Crump, would have a room next to the boys on the first floor. Now as to salary...' He mentioned a sum which made Eustacia gape at him.

'That's twice as much as I'm getting,' she told him.

'I can assure you that you will earn every penny of it. Do you know anything about little boys?'

'No, I'm afraid not.'

He smiled. 'But I believe that you would do very well with them. Will you consider it?'

She looked at her grandfather, and although he didn't say anything she saw the eagerness in his face. 'This flat?' she asked. 'It's—it's our home.'

'You could continue to rent it. Naturally I do not expect you to pay for your rooms and food at Turville.' He sounded disapproving and she blushed.

'It is a very generous offer...' she began, and he laughed then.

'My dear girl, this is no sinecure. The boot will be on the other foot if you agree to take charge of the boys. Would you like time to think it over?'

She caught sight of her grandfather's face again. 'No, thank you, sir, I shall be glad to come.' She was rewarded by the look on the old man's face. 'I shall have to give my notice. I don't know how long...?'

'Give in your notice and I'll have a word. And don't call me sir, it makes me feel old.' He got to his feet. 'I am most grateful for your help. You will hear from me as soon as the details are settled.'

She saw him to the door. 'You're quite sure...? she began as she opened it.

'Quite sure. The boys will be delighted.'

She stood in the doorway and watched him drive away and then went back to her grandfather.

He quickly dispelled any vague doubts floating around in her head. 'It couldn't be better,' he declared. 'It is a splendid start; when you leave the boys you will have a good reference and plenty of experience. You will be qualified for an even better post.'

'But Grandfather, what about you?' She sat down at the table.

'We still have this flat—there must be a job such as this one where one can live out.' He allowed himself to dream a little. 'You might even get a post in the country where there is a cottage or something similar where we might live.'

She had her doubts, but it would be unkind to throw cold water over his pleasure. She let him ramble on happily and hoped that she had done the right thing. After all, her job, although not to her liking, was, as far as she knew, safe enough, and she had earned enough to make their life a good deal easier than it had been. On the other hand, she wouldn't need to buy food, they would live rent-free and she would be able to save a good deal of the money she earned.

'I hope I'm doing the right thing,' she muttered as she went to the kitchen to get their supper.

She went to see Miss Bennett the next morning and was surprised to find that that lady knew all about it. 'You will have to work out your week's notice,' she told Eustacia, and her usually sharp voice was quite pleasant. 'There will be no difficulty in replacing you—I have a list of applicants ready to jump into your shoes.' She added even more surprisingly, 'I hope you will be happy in your new job. You will have to see the professor before you go. You are on Saturday duty this week, are you not?' And when Eustacia nodded, 'So you will leave at six o'clock on that day.'

She nodded dismissal and Eustacia escaped to the quiet of the little cubby-hole where she washed the bottles and dishes and, while she cleaned and polished, she allowed her thoughts to wander. Sir Colin hadn't said exactly when they were to go, but she hoped it wouldn't be until Monday so that she would have time to pack their things and leave the flat pristine.

There was a letter for her the following morning. If her grandfather and she could be ready by Sunday afternoon directly after lunch, they would be fetched by car and driven to Turville; he trusted that this arrangement would be agreeable to her. The letter was typewritten, but he had signed it with a scrawl which she supposed was his signature.

She could see no reason why they should not go when it was suggested, so she wrote a polite little note saying that they would be ready when the car came, and went off to tell her grandfather.

She packed their clothes on Saturday evening, got up early on Sunday morning and did some last-minute ironing, shut the cases and set about seeing that the flat was left clean. There wasn't time to cook lunch, so she opened a can of soup and made some scrambled eggs and was just nicely ready when the doorbell was rung.

She was surprised to find Sir Colin on the doorstep. He wished her good-day in his placid voice, exchanged a few words with her grandfather, helped him into the front seat and put their luggage in the boot, ushered her into the back and, without more ado, set off.

There was little traffic on the road. Just before they reached Henley, Sir Colin turned off on to a narrow road running between high hedges which led downhill into Turville. Eustacia saw with delight the black and white timbers of the Bull and Butcher Inn as they reached the village, drove round the small village green with its fringe of old cottages, past the church and down a very narrow lane with meadows on one side and a high flint wall on the other. The lane turned abruptly and they drove through an open gateway into a short, circular drive leading to a long, low house with many latticed windows and a stout wooden door, the whole enmeshed in dormant Virginia creeper, plumbago and wistaria. It would be a heavenly sight in the summer months, she thought; it was a delightful picture in mid-winter with its sparkling white paint and clay-tiled roofing. Sir Colin stopped the car before the door and it was immediately thrown open to allow the two boys to rush out, shouting with delight.

Sir Colin got out, opened Eustacia's door and helped her out, and left her to receive the exuberant greetings of the little boys while he went to help her grandfather. A grey-haired man came out of the door to join him. 'Ah, Samways, here are Mr and Miss Crump.' And, as he smiled and bowed slightly, Sir Colin went on, 'Pipe down, you two, and give a hand with the luggage.'

He had a quiet, almost placid voice and Eustacia saw that they did as they were told without demur. They all went indoors to the hall, which was wide and long with pale walls and a thick carpet underfoot. The graceful curved staircase faced them, flanked by a green baize door on the one side and on the other a glass door with a view of the garden beyond. It was pleasantly warm and fragrant with the scent of the hyacinths in the bowl on a delicate little wall-table.

Sir Colin said in his quiet voice, 'Samways, if you would show Mr Crump to his room...' He paused as the baize door opened and a small, stout woman bustled through. 'Ah, Mrs Samways, will you take Miss Crump to her room? And if we all meet for tea in ten minutes or so?'

Eustacia watched her grandfather go off happily with Samways and then, with Mrs Samways leading the way and the two boys following behind, she went up the staircase. There was a wide landing at its top with passages leading from it, and Mrs Samways took the left-hand one, to open a door at its end. 'The boys are just next door,' she explained. 'They have their own bathroom on the other side.' She led the way across the large, low-ceilinged room and opened another door. 'This is your bathroom, Miss Crump.'

It was all quite beautiful, its furniture of yew, the walls
and carpets the colour of cream, the curtains and bedspread of chintz in pale, vague colours. Eustacia was
sure that she would sleep soundly in the pretty bed, and
to wake up each morning with such a glorious view from
her windows...

'It's lovely,' she murmured, and peeped into the
bathroom, which was as charming in its way as the
bedroom with its faintly pink tiles and piles of thick
towels. She gave a sigh of pure pleasure and turned to
the boys. 'I'm glad you're next door. Do you wake
early?'

'Yes,' said Oliver, 'and now you're here, perhaps we
can go for a walk before breakfast?'

'Just listen to the boy,' said Mrs Samways comfortably, 'mad to go out so early in the day. Not that
I've anything against that, but what with getting the
breakfast and one thing and another I've not had the
time to see to them...'

'I'm sure you haven't,' said Eustacia, 'but if Sir Colin
doesn't mind and we won't be bothering you, we might
go for a quick walk as long as it doesn't upset the way
you like to run the house, Mrs Samways.'

'My dear life, it'll be a treat to have someone here to
be with the boys. Now I'll just go and fetch in the tea
and you can come down as soon as you're ready.' She
ushered the boys out ahead of her and left Eustacia,
who wasted five minutes going round her room, slowly
this time, savouring all its small luxuries: a shelf of
books, magazines on the bedside table with a tin of biscuits and a carafe of water, roomy cupboards built into
the wall, large enough to take her small wardrobe several
times over, a velvet-covered armchair by the window with
a bowl of spring flowers on a table by it. She sat down
before the triple mirror on the dressing-table and did her

face and hair and then, suddenly aware that she might be keeping everyone waiting, hurried down the stairs. The boys' voices led her to a door to one side of the hall and she pushed it open and went in. They were all in there, sitting round a roaring fire with Moses stretched out with his head on his master's feet, and a portly ginger cat sitting beside him.

Sir Colin and the boys got to their feet when they saw her, and she was urged to take a chair beside her grandfather.

'You are comfortable in your room?' asked Sir Colin.

'My goodness, yes. It's one of the loveliest rooms I've ever seen.' She beamed at him. 'And the view from the window...'

'Delightful, isn't it? Will you pour the tea, and may I call you Eustacia? The boys would like to call you that too, if you don't mind?'

'Of course I don't mind.'

She got up and went to the rent table where the tea things had been laid out, and her grandfather said, 'This is really quite delightful, but I feel that I am imposing; I have no right to be here.'

'There you are mistaken,' observed Sir Colin. 'I have been wondering if you might care to have the boys for an hour each morning. Not lessons, but if you would hear them read and keep them up to date with the world in general, and I am sure that there have been events in your life well worth recounting.'

Mr Crump looked pleased. 'As a younger man I had an eventful life,' he admitted. 'When I was in India——'

'Elephants—rajas,' chorused the boys, and Sir Colin said blandly,

'You see? They are avid for adventure. Will you give it a try?'

'Oh, with the greatest of pleasure.' Mr Crump accepted his tea and all at once looked ten years younger. 'It will be a joy to have an interest...'

Eustacia threw Sir Colin a grateful glance; he had said and done exactly the right thing, and by some good chance he had hit on exactly the right subject. Her grandfather had been in India and Burma during the 1940-45 war, and as a young officer and later as a colonel he had had enough adventures to last him a lifetime. He had stayed on in India for some years after the war had ended, for he had married while he'd been out there, and when he and her grandmother had returned to England her father had been a small schoolboy.

'I am in your debt—the boys won't be fit for school for a week or two. I hope they won't be too much of a handful for you both. It is a great relief to me that they can stay here in the country.' He looked at Eustacia. 'You won't find it too quiet here?'

She shook her head. 'Oh, no, there's such a lot to do in the country.'

They finished their tea in an atmosphere of friendly agreement, and when the tea things had been cleared away by Samways they gathered round the table and played Scrabble until Sir Colin blandly suggested that the boys should have their supper and go to bed. A signal for Eustacia to go with them, to a small, cosy room at the back of the rambling house and sit with them while they ate it. It seemed obvious to her that she was expected to take up her duties then and there, and so she accompanied them upstairs to bed after they had wished their uncle and her grandfather goodnight. Getting ready for bed was a long-drawn-out business with a great deal of toing and froing between the bathroom and their bedroom and a good deal of laughing and scampering about. But finally they were in their beds and Eustacia tucked them in, kissed them goodnight and turned off all but a small night-light by the fireplace.

'We shall like having you here,' said Oliver as she went to the door. 'We would like you to stay forever, Eustacia.'

'I shall like being here with you,' she assured him. To stay forever would be nice too, she reflected as she went to her room and tidied her hair and powdered her flushed face. She was a little surprised at the thought, a pointless one, she reminded herself, for as soon as the boys' parents returned she would have to find another job. It would be a mistake to get too attached to the children or the house. Perhaps it would be a good idea if she didn't look too far ahead but just enjoyed the weeks to come.

She went back to the drawing-room and found Sir Colin alone, and she hesitated at the door. 'Oh, I'll go and help my grandfather unpack...'

'Presently, perhaps? I shall have to leave early tomorrow morning, so we might have a little talk now while we have the opportunity.'

She sat down obediently and he got up and went over to a side-table. 'Will you have a glass of sherry?' He didn't wait for her answer, but poured some and brought it over to her before sitting down again, a glass in his hand.

'You are, I believe, a sensible young woman—keep your eye on the boys, and if you aren't happy about them, if their coughs don't clear up, let me know. Make sure that they sleep and don't rush around getting too hot. I'm being fussy, but they have had badly infected chests and I feel responsible for them. You will find the Samwayses towers of strength, but they're elderly and I don't expect them to be aware of the children's health. They are relieved that you will be here and you can call upon them for anything you may need. I shall do my best to come down at weekends and you can always phone me.'

He smiled at her, and she had the feeling that she would put up with a good deal just to please him. She squashed it immediately, for she strongly suspected that he was a man who got his own way once he had made up his mind to it.

She said in her forthright way, 'Yes, Sir Colin, I'll do my best for the boys too. Is there anything special you would want me to know about them?'

He shook his head. 'No—they're normal small boys, full of good spirits, not over-clean, bursting with energy and dreadfully untidy.'

'I've had no experience——' began Eustacia uncertainly.

'Then here is your chance. They both think you're smashing, so they tell me, which I imagine gives you the edge.'

He smiled at her very kindly and she smiled back, hoping secretly that she would live up to his good opinion of her.

Her grandfather came in then and presently they crossed the hall to the dining-room with its mahogany table and chairs and tawny walls hung with gilt-framed paintings. Eustacia sat quietly, listening to the two men talking while she ate the delicious food served to her. Mrs Samways might not be much to look at but she was a super cook.

They went back to the drawing-room for their coffee and presently she wished them goodnight and took herself off to bed, first going in search of her grandfather's room, a comfortable apartment right by the Samwayses' own quarters. He hadn't unpacked so she did that quickly, made sure that he had everything that he might need and went upstairs to her own room.

The boys were asleep; she had a bath and got into bed and went to sleep herself.

She was wakened by a plump, cheerful girl, who put a tray of tea down by the bed, told her that it was going to be a fine day and that her name was Polly, and went away again. Eustacia drank her tea with all the pleasure of someone to whom it was an unexpected luxury, put on her dressing-gown and went off to see if the boys were awake.

They were, sitting on top of their beds, oblivious to the cold, playing some mysterious game with what she took to be plastic creatures from outer space. Invited to join them, she did so and was rewarded by their loud-voiced opinions that for a girl she was quite bright, a compliment she accepted with modesty while at the same time suggesting that it might be an idea if they all had their breakfast.

She made sure that their clothes were to hand and went away to get herself dressed, and presently returned to cast an eye over hands and hair and retie shoelaces without fuss. They looked well enough, she decided, although they were both coughing. 'I'd quite like to go for a walk after breakfast,' she observed casually. 'I mean a proper walk, not on the road.'

Breakfast was a cheerful meal, with Samways hovering with porridge, bacon and scrambled eggs, and her grandfather, after a good night's sleep, willing to re-count some of his youthful adventures. Eustacia left them presently, went upstairs and made their beds and tidied the rooms, did the same for her grandfather and then went to remind the boys that they were going to take her for a walk.

'There's a windmill,' she reminded them. 'It doesn't look too far away—I'd love to see it.'

She had hit on something with which to interest them mightily. Had she seen the film *Chitty Chitty Bang Bang*? they wanted to know, because that was the very windmill in it. They walked there briskly and returned to the house for hot cocoa and an hour's reading before lunch. The afternoon was spent with her grandfather and she was able to spend an hour on her own until Mrs Samways suggested that she might like to look round the house. It was quite large and rambled a good deal. 'Rather a lot to look after,' observed Eustacia, peering at family portraits in the library.

'Ah, but there's two good girls who come up from the village each day, and Sir Colin comes mostly at weekends and then not always ... He brings a few guests from time to time and we have Christmas here, of course. He's not all that keen on London. But there he's a clever gentleman and that's where he works. I dare say if he were to marry—and dear knows I hope and pray he does, for a nicer man never stepped—he'd live here most of the time. London isn't a place for children.'

Eustacia murmured gently; she realised that Mrs Samways was doing her an honour by talking about her employer and she was glad that the housekeeper seemed to like her. It hadn't entered her head that making the beds and tidying up after the boys had endeared her to Mrs Samways' heart. 'That's a nice young lady,' she had informed her husband. 'What's more she gets on with the boys and they listen to her, more than they ever did with me.'

They had their tea in a pleasant little room at the back of the house and gathered round the table afterwards to play cards until the boys' supper and bedtime. Eustacia tucked them in finally, listening rather worriedly to their coughs, although neither of them were feverish. They had certainly eaten with youthful gusto and, by the time she had got out their clean clothes for the morning and gone to her own room to tidy herself, they were sound asleep, their nice, naughty-little-boy faces as peaceful as those of small angels.

After dinner she sat with her grandfather in the drawing-room, listening to his contented talk. He hadn't been so happy for a long time, and it reminded her of his dull existence at their flat in London; this was like a new lease of life to him. Her thoughts flew ahead to the future when the boys' parents would return and she would know that she was no longer needed. Well, she reflected, she would have to find another job similar somewhere in the country and never go back to London. She had said goodnight to her grandfather and had seen him to his room and was on the point of going upstairs when the phone rang as she was turning out the drawing-room lights.

She picked it up hesitantly, not sure if this was something the Samwayses would consider to be their prerogative, and indeed Mr Samways appeared just as she was lifting the receiver.

'I'm sorry—I should have left it for you.'

He smiled at her in a fatherly fashion. 'That's all right, miss, I dare say it will be Sir Colin.' He took the receiver from her and said in a different, impersonal voice, 'Sir Colin Crichton's residence,' and then, 'Good evening, sir. Yes, Miss Crump is here.'

He smiled again as he handed her the phone.

Sir Colin's voice came very clearly over the line. 'Eustacia? You don't mind if I call you that? The day has gone well?'

'Yes, thank you, sir. They have been very good and they went to bed and to sleep at once.' She gave him a brief, businesslike resumé of their day. 'They both cough a great deal...'

'Don't worry about that, that should clear up now they're away from London. I'll look them over when I come down. You and your grandfather have settled in?'

'Yes, thank you. Grandfather has just gone to his room. I think that he is a very happy man, sir...'

'And you, Eustacia?'

'I'm happy too, thank you, sir.'

'Good, and be kind enough to stop calling me sir with every breath.'

'Oh, very well, Sir Colin. I'll try and remember.'

He sounded as though he was laughing as he wished her goodnight and rang off.

The week went by, delightful days filled with walks, visits to the village shop, an hour or so of what Eustacia hoped was useful study with the boys and afternoons spent helping Mrs Samways with the flowers, the linen and such small tasks that the housekeeper didn't allow the maids to do, while the boys spent a blissful hour with her grandfather.

It was, thought Eustacia, too good to be true. And she was right.

Sir Colin had phoned on the Saturday morning to say that since he had an evening engagement he wouldn't be down until Sunday morning.

'I expect he's going to take Gloria out to dinner,' said Oliver. 'She's keen on him...'

Eustacia suppressed a wish to know more about Gloria and said quellingly, 'I don't think we should discuss your uncle's friends, my dear. You can stay up an hour later this evening because you always do, don't you? But no later. I dare say he'll be here quite soon after breakfast.'

The boys complained, but only mildly; she swept them upstairs to bed with only token arguments against the harshness of her edict and, with the promise that she would call them in good time in the morning just in case their uncle decided to come for breakfast, she left them to go to sleep. Her grandfather went to bed soon after them and, since there was no one to talk to and the Samwayses had gone out for the evening and wouldn't be back until late, she locked up carefully, mindful of Mr Samways' instructions about leaving the bolts undone on the garden door so that he could use his key to get in, and took herself off to bed.

She didn't hurry over her bath, and finally when she was ready for bed she opened one of the books on her bedside table, got into bed, and settled down for an hour of reading. It was an exciting book, and she was still reading it an hour later when she heard the telephone ringing.

It was almost midnight and the Samwayses weren't back yet; she bundled on her dressing-gown and went silently downstairs to the extension in the hall. She was in two minds as to whether to answer it—it was too late for a social call and it could be one of those heavy-breathing types ... She lifted the receiver slowly and said austerely, 'Yes?'

'Got you out of bed?' enquired Sir Colin. 'Eustacia, I'm now on my way to Turville. I'll be with you in half an hour. Are the Samwayses back?'

'No.' There had been something about his voice. 'Is there something the matter? Is something wrong?'

'Very wrong. I'll tell you when I get home. If you have locked up I'll come in through the garden door.'

He hung up before she could say anything more.

She left the light on in the hall and went along to the kitchen, where she put the coffee on the Aga and laid up a tray with a cup and saucer, sugar and cream, and while she did that she wondered what could have happened. An accident with his car? A medical report about one or both of the boys?

She shuffled around the kitchen, peering in cupboards looking for biscuits—he would probably be hungry. She had just found them when she heard the car, and a moment later his quiet footfall coming along the passage towards the kitchen.

He was wearing a dinner-jacket and he threw the coat he was carrying on to a chair as he came in. He nodded to her without speaking and went to warm his hands at the Aga, and when she asked, 'Coffee, Sir Colin?' he answered harshly,

'Later,' and turned to face her.

It was something terrible, she guessed, looking at his face, calm and rigid with held-back feelings. She said quietly, 'Will you sit down and tell me? You'll feel better if you can talk about it.'

He smiled a little although he didn't sit down. 'I had a telephone call just as I was about to leave my London house this evening. My brother and his wife have been killed in a car accident.'

CHAPTER THREE

EUSTACIA looked at Sir Colin in horror. 'Oh, how awful
—I am sorry!' Her gentle mouth shook and she bit her
lip. 'The boys...they're so very small.' She went up to
him and put a hand on his arm. 'Is there anything that
I can do to help?'

She looked quite beautiful with her hair loose around
her shoulders, bundled into her dressing-gown—an un-
glamorous garment bought for its long-lasting capacity—
her face pale with shock and distress, longing to comfort
him.

He looked down at her and then at her hand on his
arm. His eyes were hard and cold, and she snatched her
hand away as though she had burnt it and went to the
Aga and poured the coffee into a cup. She should have
known better, of course; she was someone filling a gap
until circumstances suited him to make other arrangements. He wouldn't want her sympathy, a stranger in
his home; he wasn't a man to show his feelings, es-
pecially to someone he hardly knew. She felt the hot
blood wash over her face and felt thankful that he
wouldn't notice it.

She asked him in her quiet voice, 'Would you like your
coffee here or in your study, Sir Colin?'

'Oh, here, thank you. Go to bed, it's late.'

She gave a quick look at his stony face and went
without a word. In her room she sat on the bed, still in
her dressing-gown, going over the past half-hour in her
mind. She wondered why she had been telephoned by
him; there had been no need, it wasn't as if he had wanted

to talk to her—quite the reverse. And to talk helped, she knew that from her own grief and shock when her parents had died. It was a pity that he had no wife in whom he could confide. There was that girl the boys had talked about, but perhaps he had been on his own when he'd had the news.

She sighed and shivered a little, cold and unhappy, and then jumped with fright when there was a tap on the door and, before she could answer it, Sir Colin opened it and came in.

He looked rigidly controlled, but the iciness had gone from his voice. 'You must forgive me, Eustacia—I behaved badly. I am most grateful for your sympathy, and I hope you will overlook my rudeness—it was unintentional.'

'Well of course it was, and there's nothing to forgive. Would you like to sit down and talk about it?' Her voice was warm and friendly, but carefully unemotional. 'It's the suddenness, isn't it?'

She was surprised when he did sit down. 'I was just leaving the house—I had a dinner date—we were standing in the hall while Grimstone, my butler, fetched my—my companion's handbag. When the phone rang I answered it but I wasn't really listening; we had been laughing about something or other. It was a long-distance call from Brunei. Whoever it was at the other end told me twice before I realised. . .' He paused, and when he went on she guessed that he was leaving something out. 'I had to get away, but I wanted to talk about it too. I got into the car and drove here and I'm not sure why I phoned you on the way.'

'Tell me about it,' said Eustacia quietly, 'and then you can decide what has to be done. Once that's settled you can sleep for a little while.'

'I shall have to fly there and arrange matters.' He glanced at his watch. 'It is too late now...'

'First thing in the morning.'

His smile shook her. 'What a sensible girl you are. I have to tell the boys before I go.' He looked at her. 'You'll stay?'

'As long as I'm needed. Tell me about your brother and his wife.'

'He was younger than I, but he married when he was twenty-three. He was an architect, a good one, with an international reputation. He and Sadie, his wife, travelled a good deal. The boys usually went with them, but this time they weren't too happy about taking them to the Far East. They were to go for three months and I had the boys—their nanny came with them but her mother was taken ill and she had to leave. Mrs Samways has done her best and so has my cook, Miss Grimstone. It was most fortunate that we made your acquaintance and that the boys took to you at once.'

'Yes. It helps, I hope. Now, we are going to the kitchen again and I'm going to make a pot of tea and a plate of toast and you will have those and then go to bed. When you've slept for a few hours you will be able to talk to the boys and arrange whatever has to be arranged.'

'You are not only sensible but practical too.'

It was after two o'clock by the time she got to bed, having made sure that Sir Colin had gone to his room. She didn't sleep for some time, and when she got up just after six o'clock she looked a wreck.

The boys were still sleeping and the house was quiet. She padded down to the kitchen and put the kettle on. A cup of tea would help her to start what was going to be a difficult day. She was warming the teapot when Sir Colin joined her. He was dressed and shaved and immaculately turned out, and he looked to be in complete control of his feelings.

'Did you sleep?' asked Eustacia, forgetting to add the 'Sir Colin' bit. And when he nodded, 'Good—will you have a cup of tea? The boys aren't awake yet. When do you plan to tell them?'

He stood there, drinking his tea, studying her; she was one of the few girls who could look beautiful in an old dressing-gown and with no make-up first thing in the morning, and somehow the sight of her comforted him. 'Could we manage to get through breakfast? If I tell them before that they won't want to eat—we must try and keep to the usual day's routine.'

'Yes, of course. May I tell Grandfather before breakfast? He is a light sleeper and there's just the chance he heard the car last night and he might mention it and wonder why you came.'

'A good point; tell him by all means. Samways will be down in a few minutes, and I'll tell him. He was fond of my brother...' He put down his cup. 'I shall be in the study if I'm wanted.'

She did the best she could to erase the almost sleepless night from her face, thankful that her grandfather had taken her news quietly and with little comment save the one that he had heard the car during the night and had known that someone was up and talking softly. Satisfied that she couldn't improve her appearance further, she went to wake the boys.

'Have you got a cold?' asked Teddy.

'Me? No. I never get colds. But I didn't go to sleep very early. I had such an exciting book...'

They discussed the pleasures of reading in bed as they dressed, and presently the three of them went downstairs and into the dining-room.

Sir Colin was sitting at the table, a plate of porridge before him, reading his post; her grandfather was leafing through the Guardian. The scene was completely normal and just for a moment Eustacia wondered if she had dreamed the night's happenings.

The boys rushed over and hugged their uncle, both talking at once. When he had come? they wanted to know. And how long was he going to stay and would he go for a walk with them?

He answered them cheerfully, begged them to sit down and eat their breakfast, bade Eustacia good morning, asked her if she would like coffee or tea and got up to fetch it for her.

Eustacia, pecking away at a breakfast she didn't want, wondered how he did it. That he was grief-stricken at the death of his brother and sister-in-law had been evident when he had talked to her but now, looking at his calm face, she marvelled at his self-control. The meal was a leisurely one and it wasn't until they had all finished that Sir Colin said, 'Eustacia, bring the boys along to the study, will you? We'll leave Mr Crump to read his paper in peace.'

He told them very simply; she marvelled at the manner in which he broke the awful news to them with a gentle gravity and a simplicity which the boys could understand. Teddy burst into tears and ran and buried his head in her lap and she held him close, but Oliver asked, 'Will they come home, Uncle?'

'Yes. I am going to fetch them.' He smiled at the child and Oliver went to him and took his hand. 'Will you look after us, Uncle? And Eustacia?'

'Of course. This will be your home and we shall be a family...'

'Mummy and Daddy wouldn't mind if you and Eustacia look after us?'

'No.' The big man's voice was very gentle. 'I think they would like that above all things.'

He put an arm round the little boy and held him close, and Eustacia, unashamedly crying while she comforted Teddy, accepted the future thrust upon her. The boys liked her, and for a time at least she could in some small way fill the immense gap in their lives. Further than that she wouldn't look for the moment.

Presently Sir Colin said, 'You know, I think a walk would do us all good. Don't you agree, Eustacia? I must get to Heathrow by two o'clock, so we can have an early lunch. I shall be gone perhaps two or three days, but you will be quite safe with Eustacia and when I get back we will have a family discussion.'

'They're safe in heaven?' Teddy wanted to know.

'Of course they are,' Sir Colin answered promptly. 'It's rather like going into another room and closing the door, if you see what I mean.'

They walked briskly up to the windmill and back again and he kept the talk deliberately on their mother and father, using a matter-of-fact tone of voice which somehow made the sadness easier to bear. Presently they sat down to an early lunch and then they waved him off in his car.

He had taken a few minutes of his time to speak to Eustacia. 'You can manage?' It was more a statement than a question. 'Very soon it will hit them hard.' His eyes searched her face. 'I believe you will be able to cope.'

She said steadily, 'Oh, yes. My parents died in a plane crash a few years ago, so I do know how they feel.'

'I didn't know. I'm sorry. You are sure...?'

'Quite sure, Sir Colin. I hope your journey will go well.'

He said softly, 'You are not only beautiful, you are a tower of strength.'

She reminded herself of that during the next few days, for just as he had warned her the boys were stricken with a childish grief, with floods of tears and wakeful nights, sudden bursts of rage and no wish to eat. It was on the third day after he had gone that he telephoned while they sat at lunch. Samways had brought the telephone to the table and given her a relieved smile. 'It's Sir Colin, Miss Crump.'

She hadn't realised just how much she had been hoping to hear from him. His voice was calm in her ear. 'Eustacia? I'm flying home in an hour's time. I'll be with you some time tomorrow. How are the boys?'

'Absolute Trojans. You'd be proud of them. Can you spare a moment to say hello?'

When they had spoken to their uncle and he had rung off, Oliver asked, 'What's a Trojan, Eustacia?'

'A very brave, strong man, my dear.'

'Like Uncle Colin?'

'Exactly like him. Aren't you lucky to have him for an uncle?'

'When I grow up,' said Teddy, 'I shall be just like him.'

'What a splendid idea, darling.'

'And I shall be like Daddy,' said Oliver, and although his lip trembled he didn't cry.

'Of course, he'll be proud of you.' She glanced at her grandfather. 'It's still raining, so how about a game of Scrabble? Let's see if we can beat Grandfather.'

She was becoming adept at keeping the boys occupied and interested. Walking, she had quickly found out, was something they liked doing, and since she had spent a good deal of her childhood in the country she was able to name birds, tell weeds from wild flowers and argue the difference between a water-vole's hole and that of a water-rat. Even on a wet morning such as it had been she managed to keep them amused, first with Scrabble and then after lunch with painting and drawing until teatime. They spent the time before bed cleaning their bikes while Eustacia did the same to Mrs Samways' elderly model, which she had been allowed to borrow. She wasn't too keen on cycling—it was years since she had ridden a bike and, although Samways had assured her that once one had learned to ride one never forgot, she wasn't too happy about it. She wasn't too happy about the skateboards either; if it was a fine morning, she had promised to try one out under the expert eyes of the boys and, although she was prepared to do anything to keep them from the grief which threatened to engulf them from time to time, she wasn't looking forward to it. But there would be no one to see her making a fool of herself, she reflected, and if she made the boys laugh so much the better.

As it turned out, she did rather better than she had expected; the boys were experts, turning and twisting with the fearlessness of the young, but they were patient with her while she wobbled her way down the slope at the back of the house, waving her arms wildly and tumbling over before she reached the bottom. They yelled and shrieked and laughed at her and did a turn themselves, showing off their expertise, and then finally she managed to reach the end of the slope still upright on her board and puffed up with pride. She did it again, only this time she began to lose her balance as she reached the end of the slope. Waving her arms wildly with the boys shouting with laughter, she fell into the arms of Sir Colin, who most fortuitously appeared at that moment to block her path. He received her person with ease, set her upright and said, 'What a nice way to be welcomed home.'

Eustacia disentangled herself, red in the face. 'Oh, we didn't know—good afternoon, Sir Colin, we're skateboarding...' She stopped, aware of a pleasant surge of delight at the sight of him and, at the same time, of the inanity of her remarks.

He didn't answer her, for the boys had rushed to meet him, and thankfully she collected the skateboards and started to walk back to the house. They would have a lot to say to each other and it would give her time to regain her normally calm manner.

Sir Colin left again on the following day; his brother had lived in London when he hadn't been travelling abroad, and his affairs had to be set in order and the funeral arranged. He told Eustacia this in an impersonal manner which didn't allow her to utter anything warmer than a polite murmur. In his calm face there was no trace of the man who had come to her room and talked as though they were friends.

'When I return we must have a talk,' he told her. 'The boys' future must be discussed.'

She was surprised that he should wish to discuss it with her; she had already said that she was willing to stay with the boys until such time as permanent arrangements had been made. Perhaps he no longer wanted her and her grandfather to remain at his house; it had been a temporary arrangement and he could hardly have envisaged their permanent residence there.

She said, 'Very well, Sir Colin,' and watched him drive away in his Rolls-Royce. There was no point in speculating about the future until he chose to tell her what he intended to do.

He returned three days later, and not alone. A middle-aged couple, his sister-in-law's parents, were with him as well as an older lady who greeted the boys with affection and then held out her hand to Eustacia.

'You must be Eustacia. My son has told me what a great help you have been to him during these last few days.'

She was tall and rather stout, but not as tall as Eustacia. She was elegantly dressed and good-looking and her eyelids drooped over eyes as blue as her son's. Eustacia liked her, but she wasn't sure that she liked the other guests. They greeted the boys solemnly and the woman burst into tears as she embraced Teddy, who wriggled in her arms.

'Mother, you have already introduced yourself—Mrs Kennedy and Mr Kennedy, my sister-in-law's parents. They will be spending a day or so here before they go back to Yorkshire.'

Clearly they regarded her as a member of the staff, nodding hastily before they turned back to the boys. Mrs Kennedy uttered little cries of, 'My poor darling boys, motherless. Oh, my dearest Sadie—the awful shock—how can I go on living? But I must, for someone must look after you...'

Mrs Crichton tapped her briskly on the shoulder. 'Dry your eyes, Freda, and endeavour to be cheerful.' She eased the two boys away from their maternal grandparents and marched them into the house. 'I'd like my tea,' Eustacia heard her say and Samways, as if on cue, appeared with a loaded tray.

Mrs Samways led the ladies away to their rooms and then Eustacia, bidden by Sir Colin, poured the tea, settled the boys with sandwiches and cake and handed plates. Mrs Crichton evinced no surprise at the sight of Eustacia sitting behind the teapot, but Mrs Kennedy raised her eyebrows and made a moue of disbelief. 'I thought this was to be a family conference,' she observed.

Sir Colin glanced at her, his face blandly polite, his eyes hidden by the heavy lids. 'Which it is, but I think we might have tea first. Mr Baldock will be here very shortly with Peter's will. In the meanwhile shall we hear what the boys have been doing with themselves?' He glanced at Eustacia. 'Any more walks to the windmill?'

She nodded. 'Oliver, do tell about the rabbits...'

He embarked on a long account of the animals they had seen and Teddy, his tears forgotten, joined in. 'And we had another go with the skateboards,' said Oliver. 'Eustacia stayed on twice, she's not bad for a girl.'

Mrs Kennedy drew a deep breath. 'But surely, today of all days, they should have been——?'

She wasn't allowed to finish—Mrs Crichton said rapidly, 'I've always wanted to go on one of those things. Is it difficult, Eustacia?'

'Very, Mrs Crichton, but such fun. The boys are very good, I don't know who showed them how—Sir Colin, perhaps?'

She hadn't meant the question seriously, but he answered at once. 'Indeed I did. I consider myself pretty good. Once we have perfected Eustacia's technique I think we must persuade Mr and Mrs Samways...'

A remark which set the boys rolling around with laughter, and Mrs Kennedy's expression became even more disapproving. She looked at her husband, who cleared his throat and began, 'The boys——' but got no further, for Samways announced Mr Baldock.

He was elderly, tall and thin and wore old-fashioned pince-nez attached to his severe black coat by a cord, but his eyes were very alive and he had a surprisingly loud voice. Sir Colin got up to greet him while Samways fetched fresh tea. 'You know everyone, I believe, except Miss Eustacia Crump, who is my right hand and a tower of strength and common sense.'

He shook her hand and took a good look at her. 'A very pretty name and certainly a very pretty girl,' he

observed. 'You are indeed fortunate.' He added
thoughtfully, 'Small boys can be the very devil.'

She agreed composedly. 'But they are great fun too—
they see things one overlooks when one is grown-up.'

'Intelligent, too.' He sat down, accepted a cup of tea
and made light conversation about this and that, never
once alluding to the funeral they had all attended earlier
that day. Not an easy matter, for Mrs Kennedy tried her
best to turn the cheerful tea-party into a wake.

Tea things cleared, Eustacia rose, intent on making
an unobtrusive exit with the boys. She was hindered,
however, by Sir Colin. 'Take the boys along to Mrs
Samways, Eustacia, and come back here, will you?'

She gave him an enquiring look and he smiled and
added, 'Please?'

She slipped back into the room and Sir Colin looked
round and smiled again as she sat down a little to one
side of the gathering.

'Good. Will you start, Mr Baldock?' Sir Colin sat
back, his long legs stretched out before him, and smiled
at his mother.

The will was brief and very much to the point. Sir
Colin was to be the legal guardian of Oliver and Teddy,
assisted as he might think fit by some suitable person or
persons and should he marry it was hoped that his wife
would become a guardian also. The bulk of the estate
went to the boys in trust, but there were legacies for
members of the family and various directions as to the
selling of property.

Mr Baldock smoothed the pages neatly and took off
his pince-nez. 'A very sensible document, if I may be
allowed to say so. And quite straightforward.'

'But it's ridiculous,' exclaimed Mrs Kennedy. 'I have
every right to have the boys, they are my
grandchildren——'

'They are also mine,' said Mrs Crichton briskly, 'but I don't consider that any of us has a right to them. Colin is very well fitted to bring them up, and if he should marry they will have brothers and sisters as any normal child would like to have.'

'But Colin has no time—he's at that hospital all hours of the day and he's always travelling from one place to another; the boys will be left to servants——'

'They will be in the care of Eustacia, whom they happen to have developed a deep affection for. She has promised to stay and care for them and, despite my work, I do spend my evenings and nights at home. As soon as they are perfectly fit they will go back to school like any other small boys, and if it is possible they will come with me should I have a lecture tour or seminars.'

'And this—this Eustacia? Will she go with you?' Mrs Kennedy was plum-coloured with temper.

He gave her a cold look from eyes suddenly icy. 'Of course. Much as I enjoy their company, I am not conversant with their wants. If Mr Baldock agrees to this arrangement as the other executor of the will, I think that it will work perfectly.'

'Do you intend to marry in the foreseeable future?' asked Mr Kennedy.

Sir Colin said, 'Yes,' without a moment's hesitation, and Eustacia felt a distinct pang of regret. And very silly too—she gave herself a metaphorical shake—there was no earthly reason why she should concern herself with Sir Colin's private life.

'And until such time as this should occur,' said Mr Baldock, 'you are willing to remain as surrogate mother to Oliver and Teddy?' He studied her over his glasses and gave a little nod of approval.

'Yes, I told Sir Colin that I would stay as long as I am needed, and if you wish me to do so I will repeat my promise.'

'No need, my dear young lady. I perceive that you are eminently suitable for the post.' He glanced across to Mrs Crichton. 'You agree with me, Mrs Crichton?'

'Absolutely. And I am sure that Mr and Mrs Kennedy will give their approval. The boys are fortunate in having grandparents living in such a lovely part of Yorkshire— think of the holidays they will enjoy...'

Mrs Kennedy dabbed her eyes with a handkerchief. 'I still think that it is against human nature...'

Everyone looked rather puzzled until Sir Colin said kindly, 'But you must agree that Peter—and I'm sure that Sadie would have agreed with him—was thinking of the boys and their future. I must state the obvious and point out that when they are still young men I shall, hopefully, be here to act as their guardian, whereas you may no longer be with us.'

'Well, really,' exclaimed Mrs Kennedy, 'what a thing to say.' She caught her husband's eye. 'Though that may be true enough. They must come to us for holidays.'

'Of course, and you both know that you are always welcome at my home. I was fond of Sadie and it is a consolation to know that they were devoted to each other and the boys. We must all do our best to continue that devotion.'

From anyone else it would have sounded pompous, reflected Eustacia, but Sir Colin had uttered the words in a calm and unhurried voice and moreover had sounded quite cheerful.

'Eustacia, would you fetch the boys here, please? And how about a drink before dinner? You'll stay, of course, Mr Baldock? Samways will drive you back to town.'

Eustacia ushered the boys into the drawing-room and slid away to find her grandfather. He was in his room, sitting before a cosy little fire, enjoying a late tea. He bent a patient ear to her account of the family gathering and agreed with her that she had no option but to stay with the boys.

'Their granny and grandpa from Yorkshire don't like the idea,' she explained, 'they don't like me; they want the boys with them but they had to agree to the will. I don't think Sir Colin's mother minds; she's nice and she's sad, but she didn't let the boys see that...'

She went away presently to be told that as a great treat the boys were to stay up for dinner. Sir Colin, when he told her, didn't mention that Mrs Kennedy had expressed annoyance at the idea of Eustacia's dining with them; she had made the mistake of saying so in front of the boys, who had instantly chorused that if Eustacia couldn't be there, they didn't want to be there either.

Sir Colin, a tactful man, smoothed frayed tempers and presently they all sat down to dinner, during which he kept the conversation firmly in his hands, aided by his mother, not allowing Mrs Kennedy to dwell on the unhappy circumstances which had brought them together that day. And after the meal, when Eustacia had bidden everyone goodnight and borne the boys off to their beds, he played the perfect host until Mr Baldock declared that he must go home and Mr and Mrs Kennedy retired to bed, for they were to stay the night. Only when he was alone with his mother did Sir Colin allow his bland mask to fall.

'Not the happiest of days, my dear,' he observed. 'I would wish that we could have been alone—there has been no chance to talk about Peter. I shall miss him and so will you. You have been very brave, Mother, and a great help. It is a pity that the Kennedys can't see that the boys are more important than anything else.'

'I never liked the woman,' said Mrs Crichton forth-rightly. 'I like that young woman, Eustacia, and the boys like her too. She will be able to give them the comfort they'll need. I must get to know her.' She stood up. 'I'm going to bed now, my dear—don't sit here grieving.'

He stood up and kissed her cheek. 'You'll stay a few days? I'll be free at the weekend, and I'll run you back to Castle Cary—the boys will enjoy the ride.'

At breakfast he was his usual pleasant self, joking with the boys, exchanging opinions with Mr Kennedy about the day's news and listening courteously to Mrs Kennedy's advice about the boys' coughs. Eustacia, watching him when she could, saw the tired lines in his face and the tiny muscle twitching in his cheek. Probably he had slept badly and no wonder, he had had a wretched week and hadn't complained once. That bland, cheerful manner must have cost him something... He looked up and caught her eye and smiled warmly and her heart gave a lurch and she glanced away, feeling uncertain and not knowing why.

The Kennedys went presently after a protracted farewell to the boys, a chilly one to Sir Colin and his mother and a frosty nod to Eustacia. Quite definitely she wasn't liked.

With their departure it was as though a cloud had lifted from the house. Sir Colin stayed for lunch and then went back to the hospital, saying as he went that he would be back at the weekend. 'We'll take Granny back home and see about Moses's leg on Sunday—that plaster is due to come off.'

He kissed his mother, gave the boys an avuncular hug and opened his car door, then turned back to where they were standing outside the door to wave him on his way.

'You will phone me if you are in the least worried about anything, Eustacia.' She was surprised when he went and kissed her swiftly, then he got into his car and drove away.

Eustacia had gone delightfully pink, but a quick glance at her companions showed her that they had either not noticed or they found nothing strange in Sir Colin's behaviour. They went into the house and she told herself that he had been acting out of kindness, not wishing her to feel left out. He had certainly noticed Mrs Kennedy's coldness towards her although he had said nothing.

Mrs Crichton took the boys to the village shop to buy sweets, and Eustacia went along to see her grandfather. He looked up with a smile as she joined him.

'Sir Colin gone? But back at the weekend, he tells me. You are quite happy about this job, my dear? I must say that Mrs Kennedy didn't seem too pleased about it, but really it is a most sensible arrangement at least until such time as the boys are over their grief. Thank heaven that children are so resilient. Am I to continue with our little sessions or are they to be free?'

Eustacia sat down beside him. 'I should think that an hour in the afternoon would be a good idea. Mrs Crichton will be here for the rest of the week and I think she might like to have them to herself in the mornings. She's very fond of them and they love her.'

'A fine woman, and she has a fine son.'

The week passed pleasantly and Eustacia took care to fill the days so that the boys had no time to mope. There were moments of sadness, but comforting and some small treat mitigated those and Mrs Crichton was a great help; she had her son's calmness and a capacity for inventing interesting games. She and Eustacia liked each other and, with her grandfather and the faithful Samways backing them up, Eustacia felt that they had come through a trying two weeks very well.

Sir Colin arrived home on Friday evening. The boys were already in bed but Eustacia, crossing the hall on the way to the dining-room with a tray of glasses as he came in, paused to say that they were still awake and waiting for him.

He crossed the hall, took the tray from her and said, 'Good. How are they?'

'Recovering well. Mrs Crichton has been marvellous with them and they love her very much, don't they?'

'Yes. Why are you carrying trays?'

'Just one tray, Sir Colin. Samways is in the cellar and Mrs Samways can't leave the stove just at the moment.' She took the tray back. 'Your mother is in the drawing-room.'

He nodded and looked faintly amused. 'You will join us with your grandfather? He is well?'

'Yes. Thank you. The boys have had their reading lessons and they're starting on a map of India.'

'Splendid.'

He let her go then and went unhurriedly into his drawing-room where his mother and Moses waited for him.

She was told at breakfast the next day that she would be going to Castle Cary with the boys—something she hadn't expected. 'We'll leave directly after we have had coffee, stop for lunch on the way, have tea there and drive back in the early evening.'

An announcement hailed with delight by the boys and uncertainty by Eustacia.

'Oh, very well, Sir Colin, but I thought you might like to have the boys...'

He smiled his kind smile. 'I'm delighted to have the boys; I'm not sure if I'm qualified to cope with their various needs. Your grandfather assures me that he will very much enjoy a day on his own. The Samwayses will take good care of him.'

They drove down to Henley-on-Thames, through Wokingham and on to the M3, and presently they were on the A303. At Amesbury they stopped for lunch at the Antrobus Hotel, a pleasantly old-fashioned hotel where the boys were listened to with sympathy when they requested sausages and some chips in preference to the more sophisticated menu.

It was a cheerful meal, and they drove on in high spirits until they reached Wincanton and turned off to Castle Cary. Eustacia had never been there and she was enchanted by the mellow stone cottages and the narrow high street lined with small shops.

Mrs Crichton lived in the centre of the small town, in a large Georgian house with a vast front door with its brass knocker and bell. There was no garden before it but the windows were just too high for passers-by to peer in. In any case, Eustacia thought, it was such a dignified house, no one would dare to stare in even if they could.

The door was opened as they got out of the car and a small, stout woman ushered them in, beaming from a rosy-cheeked elderly face.

'Well, madam dear, it's nice to see you back and no mistake. And the two young gentlemen too, and how is Mr Colin?'

'All the better for seeing you, Martha.' He placed a kiss on her cheek. 'This is Eustacia Crump, who is looking after the boys. Eustacia, this is Martha, who has lived with us forever.'

They shook hands and liked each other at once. 'Now, isn't that nice?' observed Martha in her soft Somerset voice.

The house was warm and very welcoming; it was furnished with some lovely old pieces and yet it was lived in and comfortable. Mrs Crichton led the way into a high-ceilinged room overlooking the street. 'I know you can't stay long, but tea will only be a few minutes.'

Eustacia took the boys' coats and caps, took off her own coat and went with them to look at the garden from the big bay window of a room leading out of the sitting-room. It was rather grandly furnished and a Siamese cat was sitting on the rent table by the window. It got up sedately and went to meet Mrs Crichton and they all gathered by the window to look at the garden. It was large, charmingly laid out and walled. Even with local traffic going to and fro the house was very quiet.

'You must come and stay when the weather is warmer,' said Mrs Crichton. 'The Easter holidays, perhaps?' An invitation accepted with enthusiasm by the boys. Eustacia shared their enthusiasm but she didn't say so—she wasn't sure if she was included in the invitation.

They had their tea in a small room at the back of the hall, at a round table near the open fire. The kind of tea little boys liked: muffins swimming in butter, Marmite on toast cut in little fingers, fruit cake and sandwiches and a plate of chocolate biscuits to finish. The boys ate with gusto and so, for that matter, did Sir Colin.

They left soon after tea and this time the boys were strapped into the back seats and Eustacia was bidden to sit in front.

The boys were sleepy by the time they got back; they ate their supper quickly, full of their day and the pleasure of taking Moses to the vet in the morning, but they were too tired to protest when Eustacia bade them say good-night to their uncle and whisked them upstairs to baths and bed. When she got down again, it was to find Sir Colin gone. An urgent call from St Biddolph's, Samways told her, and he would see her at breakfast. She dined with her grandfather, recounting details of their trip while they ate.

'You didn't mind being on your own, Grandfather?'

'My dear child, it was delightful. I had the leisure to read and write and eat the delicious meals Mrs Samways cooked. I have never been more content. I realise that it cannot last forever, but I am grateful for these weeks of pleasant living.'

They went to the vet's in the morning and Moses had his plaster removed and was allowed, cautiously, to walk on all his legs. After lunch, since Sir Colin said that he had work to do in his study, Eustacia took the boys for a ride on their bikes, mounting guard upon them from the elderly bike which Mrs Samways had lent to her.

They all had tea round the fire and then a rousing game of Snap before the boys had supper and went to bed. Eustacia came down presently to find Sir Colin and her grandfather discussing the boys' schooling, but they broke off when she joined them and Sir Colin got up to fetch her a drink.

'I think that the boys might go back to school in another two weeks,' he told her. 'There is a good prep school on the other side of Turville Heath, only a mile or so away. Can you drive, Eustacia?'

'Yes, but I haven't for several years.'

'Well, there is a Mini in the garage—take it out once or twice and see how you get on. Samways will go with you if you like.'

'I'd rather go alone.'

'I shall be away all this next week but here for the weekend. The following week I have to go to Leiden to give a series of lectures. I'll leave a phone number in case of an emergency but you will find Samways a tower of strength. Your grandfather has most kindly suggested that he should have the boys each morning for easy-going lessons so that they won't feel too strange when they start school.'

They dined in a leisurely fashion, and later when she said goodnight he said, 'I shall be gone by the time you get down in the morning. Enjoy your week, Eustacia.'

She did; the boys had recovered their good spirits and she kept them occupied when they weren't at their lessons. She thought the lessons weren't very serious, for she heard gales of laughter coming from the room where they studied with her grandfather. She told Samways that she was to drive the Mini and he got it from the garage for her and told her of the quietest roads. After the first uncertain minutes, she found that she was enjoying herself hugely. After the first day or two she ventured on to a nearby main road and then drove to the school where the boys were to go, quite confident now.

When Sir Colin came at the weekend she assured him that she felt quite capable of driving the boys, and he said at once, 'Good. Get your coat, we'll go over to the school—I want to see the headmaster.'

Something she hadn't bargained for, but she got into the driver's seat, and since she was a big girl and he was an extremely large man the journey was a cramped one— indeed she found it rather unsettling.

At Sir Colin's request, she went with him and was introduced. 'So that you are known here when you come to fetch the boys,' explained Sir Colin. They went back home presently; the boys were to start school in two weeks' time—after half-term—and she would fetch them each day and ferry them to and fro.

The weekend went too quickly and on Monday morning Sir Colin left again. 'I'll be away for a week, perhaps a little longer—I have friends in Holland and I may stay a day or two with them.'

He hugged the boys, promised that he would bring them something Dutch when he got back, shook Mr Crump's hand and, rather as an afterthought, kissed Eustacia's cheek before he drove himself off.

The house seemed empty without him; he was a quiet man but somehow, reflected Eustacia, one felt content and secure when he was there. The days ahead looked empty. She was vexed with herself for feeling discontented—the calm routine of their days was something to be thankful for.

It was towards the middle of the week that the calm was disrupted.

Mrs Kennedy telephoned quite late one evening; the boys were long since in bed and her grandfather had gone to his room.

'I wish to speak to Sir Colin,' said Mrs Kennedy. 'Is that the maid?'

'Eustacia,' said Eustacia with polite coolness.

Mrs Kennedy gave a nasty little laugh. 'Well, fetch him, will you?'

'He isn't here, Mrs Kennedy.'

'Oh, where is he? In town?'

'He's abroad.' The moment she had said it, Eustacia would have given anything to recall her words.

'Do you mean to say that he has left you in charge of my grandsons? You're not capable of looking after them. I simply won't have it.' She was fast working herself into a temper. 'I don't know how long he will be away but I intend fetching them to stay with us until such time as he returns. It was made clear in my son-in-law's will that they should live with their guardian, but obviously Sir Colin chose to ignore that. Expect me some time tomorrow and have the boys ready to leave with us.'

She hung up abruptly and Eustacia replaced the receiver.

It was time-wasting to call herself a fool, but she undoubtedly was. What was more she was shaking with fright and rage. She must do something about it, and quickly. She went to Sir Colin's study and took the slip of paper from his desk, and picked up the phone and dialled the number on it.

She was answered very quickly but she had to wait until he was found. His 'Yes, Eustacia?' was uttered in a calm voice which checked her wild wish to burst into tears and, while she was struggling for a normal voice, he said, 'Take your time and try not to cry.'

She took a deep breath and, in a voice squeaky with battened-down emotions, began to speak.

CHAPTER FOUR

'MRS KENNEDY,' said Eustacia in a voice she was pleased to hear sounded normal. 'She telephoned about ten minutes ago; she asked to speak to you and I said you weren't here, so she asked where you were.' She gulped. 'I said that you were abroad, and do call me fool if you want to because that's what I am... She said that I wasn't fit to look after the boys and they should be living with her because you weren't at home, and she is coming to fetch them tomorrow...'

'Dear me, what a tiresome lady, and don't reproach yourself, Eustacia, you weren't to know that she was going to turn nasty. Now please stop worrying about it; I'll be home in time to deal with the matter. Go to bed, there's a good girl.' He sounded just as he did when he was talking to his nephews: firm but kind.

'But you're in Holland—it's miles away...'

'Have you never heard of aeroplanes, Eustacia? Are you crying?'

'Well, a bit—I've let you down.'

'Don't be silly; now go to bed. Oh, and unbolt the garden door again, will you? Leave it locked and take the key out of the lock.'

She dealt with the door and went obediently to bed where, surprisingly, she slept until the early morning. She lay and worried for a while and then got up, showered and dressed and crept downstairs with the vague idea that, if Mrs Kennedy should arrive unexpectedly, she would at least be ready for her. She gained the bottom of the staircase and the study door opened and Sir Colin came out. He was dressed with his usual elegance and from where she was standing he appeared to be a man who had had a good night's sleep in his bed.

She surged across the hall, delight and relief making her beautiful face a sight to linger over. 'Oh, you're here, I'm so very glad to see you.'

He smiled down at her. 'Good morning, Eustacia. Why are you up and dressed at six o'clock in the morning?'

She answered him seriously. 'Well, I thought if Mrs Kennedy arrived unexpectedly I'd be ready for her.'

'I told you I would be home in time to see her.'

'Yes, and I believed you, but you might need help.'

His eyes gleamed with amusement but he said gravely, 'That was most thoughtful of you. Do you suppose we might have a cup of tea?'

'Of course, I'll bring you a tray. Would you like some toast with it?'

'Yes, I would. We will have it in the kitchen while we make our plans.'

The kitchen was warm, and Moses opened a sleepy eye and thumped his tail with pleasure at seeing his master. Eustacia put the kettle on the Aga and fetched cups and saucers while Sir Colin cut the bread.

'Is there any of Mrs Samways' marmalade?' he wanted to know, and loaded the toaster. She found the marmalade and the butter and got plates and knives and presently they sat down opposite each other at the big scrubbed table with Moses sitting as close as he could get to Sir Colin.

'How did you get here so quickly? There aren't any planes during the night, are there?'

'I chartered one.' He took a bite of toast.

'Oh, I see. You didn't mind me phoning you, Sir Colin? It hasn't made a mess of your seminar—or was it lectures?'

He smiled. 'Both, and the lectures were finished—the seminar isn't all that important.' He passed his cup for more tea. 'No, I didn't mind your phoning, Eustacia; indeed, I would have been very angry if you hadn't.'

'It was silly of me...'

'Why? You were not to know what Mrs Kennedy intended.'

'What shall you do?' She passed the marmalade. 'She can't take the boys away, can she?'

'Of course not.' He sounded placid. 'And there is a simple solution to the problem.'

'Oh—good.' She bent to give Moses a piece of buttered toast.

'We could marry.'

She almost choked on her toast. 'Marry? You and me? Me? Marry you?'

'A very sensible idea,' he pointed out smoothly. 'You will then be a guardian of the boys and there can never be a question of their being taken away from us.'

'But I don't—that is, you don't...' She came to a stop searching for the right words.

'I hardly see that that comes into it. We get on well together, do we not? We should be able to provide a secure background for the boys without getting emotionally involved with each other. After all, there won't be any difference if you become my wife; we get along well, as I have just said, and I see no reason why we shouldn't continue to do so. I am a good deal older than you and there is always the hazard that you may meet someone with whom you will fall in love, in which case the situation can be dealt with reasonably. I assure you that I wouldn't stand in your way.'

It sounded very cold and businesslike. 'Supposing you fall in love?' she asked him.

'But I already have, so you need not concern yourself with that.'

'Grandfather...?'

'A delightful old gentleman, welcome to live here for the remainder of his days.'

'I—I would like to think about it.' There was a panicky excitement inside her.

'By all means,' he glanced at his watch, 'I doubt if the Kennedys will get here for another two hours at the earliest.'

'You mean I have to decide before then?'

'It would make things much easier.' He smiled across the table; he was tired but he knew exactly what he was doing. 'Do you suppose your grandfather is up yet? I should like to talk to him.'

She was glad to have an excuse to get away. Her head was in a turmoil and she simply had to have time to think. 'I'll go and see. I think he may be in the library— he likes to read before breakfast.'

She left the two men there and went to get the boys out of their beds.

'You look funny,' said Oliver as she brushed his hair. In case she hadn't understood, he added, 'You're pretty, I don't mean that—you look excited.'

'Probably the thought of breakfast. I'm hungry, aren't you?'

'Yes!' shouted Teddy. 'Bacon and eggs and sausages and mushrooms and toast and marmalade...'

The three of them hurried downstairs.

Over breakfast Mr Crump suggested that since their uncle was home and might want to take them out later it would be a good idea if they did some reading first.

'What a splendid idea,' observed Sir Colin, for all the world as though he hadn't just arranged that, and smiled at Eustacia. He looked pleased with himself and confident, as though he was certain that she would consent to his preposterous idea. She would have to talk to him about it once the boys had gone with her grandfather, but as it turned out she had no chance—they had left the table, the boys and Mr Crump to go to the library, she to make the beds upstairs, Sir Colin presumably to go about his own business, when there was a demanding peal on the doorbell.

Sir Colin caught her by the arm as Samways went to answer it.

'Mrs Kennedy?' she heard him say to Samways, who nodded with dignity and a knowing look. So Sir Colin had found time to tell Samways too... Eustacia allowed herself to be drawn into the drawing-room. 'Sit there,' said Sir Colin and urged her into a small easy-chair facing the door, 'and don't say a word unless I ask you something.' He smiled suddenly. 'Will you marry me, Eustacia?'

She opened her mouth to explain that she must have time to think about it, but now there were voices, rather loud, in the hall—any moment Mrs Kennedy and Mr Kennedy with her would be in the room. She said snappily, 'Oh, all right, but I haven't——' She felt the quick kiss on her cheek and then he was gone, to the other end of the room away from the door, where he wouldn't be seen at once.

Samways opened the door and Mrs Kennedy and her husband surged past him, ignoring his announcement.

'It has been no easy matter driving here, Miss—er—Crump, but I know my duty. If Sir Colin feels unable to make a suitable home for the boys then I must sacrifice my time and leisure and bring them up as befits my daughter's children. Be good enough to send for Oliver and Teddy at once; they will return with us. When Sir Colin chooses to return we can discuss the matter further. For them to remain here with nothing but a parcel of servants is quite——' She stopped, her cross face assuming a look of utter astonishment, her eyes popping.

Sir Colin had advanced a few steps so that he had come into her line of vision. His voice was blandly polite. 'Mrs Kennedy, you must have had a very tiring journey— you travelled through the night? May I offer you both breakfast?'

Mrs Kennedy made a gobbling noise. 'She,' she nodded at Eustacia, 'told me that you were abroad.'

'Eustacia spoke the truth; when you telephoned I was. It seemed to me to be necessary to come home and put your mind at rest about the boys. Let me allay your doubts—Eustacia and I are to be married very shortly so that, when I need to be away from home, they will have a guardian in her.'

'Marry her?' Mrs Kennedy had gone an unbecoming plum colour.

Sir Colin's voice was as steely as his eyes. 'Eustacia has done me that honour.'

'It's a put-up job, she's no more——'

'I beg your pardon, Mrs Kennedy?'

Mr Kennedy spoke for the first time. 'My wife didn't mean that,' he said hastily. 'I did explain to her that everything was quite satisfactory as regards the boys.' He added awkwardly, 'My congratulations, I hope you will be very happy.'

Mrs Kennedy had pulled herself together. 'Yes, yes indeed. I spoke hastily. One forgets how quickly one can travel these days. Aeroplanes, you know, and hovercraft and so on.' She looked around her a little wildly and

Eustacia, much as she disliked her, decided that it was time to rescue her from an awkward situation.

'Won't you sit down, Mrs Kennedy and Mr Kennedy? And shall I fetch the boys, Colin?'

She uttered this in what she hoped was a sufficiently loving voice and got answered in her own coin.

'Will you, darling? And ask Samways to bring coffee, would you?'

The smile which went with it was full of tender charm as he went to open the door for her. She didn't dare to look at him. He must be a splendid actor, she reflected, hurrying across the hall; she had read somewhere that surgeons very often had a strong artistic streak, and his must be acting.

The boys weren't exactly enthusiastic. 'Must we?' asked Oliver. 'Mr Crump was just telling us about the Aztecs and it's really very interesting.'

'Yes, I'm sure it is,' agreed Eustacia, 'and you won't need to stay long. I'm sure Grandfather will be delighted to continue when you get back. He's going to have a cup of coffee now.'

The boys behaved beautifully, offering hands and cheeks and answering politely when they were questioned. They pretended not to notice when their grandmother started crying, and Eustacia suggested that she might like to freshen up after her drive. A sudden imp of mischief prompted her to add, 'Perhaps you would like to stay the night?' She turned her beautiful face towards Sir Colin. 'Don't you think that is a good idea, Colin?' She gave him an innocent look, and he turned a sudden laugh into a fit of coughing.

'By all means, darling.' He sounded the perfect host, anxious to do all he could for his guests.

However, the Kennedys didn't wish to stop. Mrs Kennedy was shepherded away to repair her face and tidy herself, and presently they made their farewells and drove away with the assurance, not over-enthusiastically received by them, that Sir Colin, Eustacia and both the boys would spend a day or two with them as soon as the warmer weather arrived.

They stood on the steps, waving, and the two boys scampered back to Mr Crump. 'I had no idea that you had it in you, Eustacia,' said Sir Colin.

'Had what, Sir Colin?'

'This ability to be a loving fiancée at a moment's notice, although I could have wished for a few more melting glances.'

'Well, I didn't want to overdo it.'

'That would be impossible.' He turned her round and took her arm and walked her into the house. 'Now, when shall we get married?'

She turned to face him. 'You aren't serious?' She studied his face and decided that he was.

'Am I to be jilted before we are even engaged? I had thought better of you, Eustacia.'

She stammered a little. 'I thought—well, I thought that it was just an emergency.'

'Certainly not—an expediency, perhaps. You must see, since you are a sensible girl, that if we marry it ensures a secure and happy future for the boys with no further interference from the Kennedys. Of course, they have every right to see the boys as often as they wish, and have them to stay for holidays, but this will be their home and you and I will be, in effect, their parents.'

She had nothing to say; it all sounded so logical and businesslike.

Sir Colin eyed her thoughtfully. 'Naturally our marriage will be one of convenience. We have, I think, a mutual liking for each other which is more than can be

said of a good many marriages these days. Should you
meet a man you truly love, then I will release you——'

'And what about you?' asked Eustacia sharply.
'You're just as likely to meet another woman.'

He said seriously, 'I'm thirty-six, my dear, I have had
every opportunity to meet another woman...'

'What about Gloria?'

She wished she hadn't said it, for his face became as
bland as the voice with which he echoed her. 'Gloria?'

She muttered, 'It was something I heard, and I thought
that she was——'

'Set your mind at rest, Eustacia. Gloria was—still is—
a friend of long standing and the very last woman I would
marry.'

She went pink but met his look candidly. 'I'm sorry,
it isn't my business—it was impertinent of me.'

The bland look which she didn't much care for disappeared and he smiled at her, the kind smile which made
her feel that everything was all right between them. He
said gently, 'I am a good deal older than you, Eustacia—
if you do have second thoughts I shall understand.'

'Well, I hadn't thought about it,' she told him, 'and
it doesn't matter. I do like you very much and I think
that I could love the boys, really love them, and I should
be very happy living here with them...'

He chuckled. 'I do come home at weekends and
sometimes during the week. Besides, from time to time
I should like you to come up to town. I have many friends
and I like to entertain them occasionally. Have you any
objection to that?'

'Me? No, it sounds exciting. You don't mind
Grandfather being here? Would you like him to go back
to the flat? I dare say——'

'Certainly not. I find him a delightful man and the
boys like the time they spend with him and are fond of

him. I believe he is happy here, is he not? And he is performing a yeoman service teaching them to play chess and answering all their questions, and I suspect that when they go to school he will be roped in to help them with their homework.'

They had been standing in the hall, and at Samways' little cough they both looked round.

'I thought perhaps some fresh coffee, sir?'

'Excellent, Samways. And please fetch up a couple of bottles of champagne—we will have some at lunch. Miss Crump and I have just become engaged.'

Samways was delighted; he offered congratulations with suitable gravity, mentioned that Mrs Samways would be more than pleased to hear the news, and went away to fetch the coffee.

'I think,' said Sir Colin, sitting in his chair with a coffee-cup in his hand, 'that you had better come up to town with me; I have a small house there, and I should like you to meet Grimstone who runs it for me—his sister does the cooking. We must decide on a date for the wedding too.' He sat thinking. 'I'm rather busy for the next few days but I will send Samways down to fetch my mother—she can stay here and help your grandfather to keep an eye on the boys so that you may spend a few days shopping. Would you object to marrying here in the village? The church is rather nice...'

Really, thought Eustacia, he's arranged everything in a couple of sentences. She said calmly, 'I think that would be delightful—being married here, I mean. And if you want me to come up to London with you then I will. The boys will be all right?'

'Perfectly all right. We will drive up this afternoon and I'll bring you back this evening. I have a list in the morning but not until ten o'clock, so I can spend the night.' He glanced at her. 'Am I going too fast for you?'

'Yes, but I'll catch up. Will your mother mind?'

'No. She likes you. Shall we go and tell your grandfather and the boys?'

Their news was received with boisterous delight by the boys and quiet satisfaction by her grandfather.

'You'll never go away?' asked Teddy. 'You'll look after us?'

She hugged him. 'Of course I will, we'll all have such fun...'

'And when you're an old lady,' said Oliver, 'if you need looking after, you and Uncle Colin, we'll take care of you both.'

'I think we shall both be very glad to have you around and it is very kind of you to think of us, my dear.'

'We call Uncle Colin Uncle—do we have to call you Aunt?'

'Only if you would like to.'

'You won't mind if we call you Eustacia?'

'I should like it above all things.'

She had sat down at the table with the boys on either side of her, and Sir Colin turned round from the conversation he was having with her grandfather.

'Uncle Colin, we think you are a very lucky man,' said Oliver.

'I know I am, old chap. We shall be married here quite soon and have all our friends at the church.'

'And a cake, and Eustacia will be a bride in a white dress?'

Before she could answer, Sir Colin said positively, 'Yes, to both questions.'

'A party?' asked Teddy, happily.

'A party it shall be.' He spoke to his small nephew but he looked at Eustacia, smiling faintly. Quite carried away by the excitement of the moment, she smiled back, her cheeks pink and her eyes sparkling.

The next hour or so seemed a little hazy, partly due to the champagne and the children's excitement, which made sensible conversation, or sensible thought for that matter, impossible. Presently she found herself sitting beside Sir Colin, in the Rolls, waving goodbye to the little group at the front of the house, and when they were out of sight she sat back composedly, very neat in the elderly suit. There was still a great deal she wanted to know and she supposed she would be told sooner or later; meanwhile there seemed little point in aimless chatter.

Presently Sir Colin said, 'It is the prerogative of the bride to decide what kind of wedding she wants, is it not? There was no chance to explain my high-handed plans, but perhaps you understood?'

'Yes. It's for the boys, isn't it? It will help them to adjust, won't it? If they have something positive to hang on to.'

'Exactly. This afternoon we are going to visit an old friend of my father's. He is a bishop and I hope he will be able to advise us about a special licence and the quickest way to get one. I shall put an announcement in the *Telegraph* tomorrow and invite friends to the wedding. I haven't many relations, but they will come, I'm sure of that. So will colleagues I work with. Is there anyone you would like to invite? I know that you have no family...'

'There isn't anyone—I had friends, but during the last two years I've lost touch.'

'I dare say one or two people from the path lab will want to come.'

They were in London by now, going through Chiswick and Kensington and skirting Hyde Park, up Park Lane and then into the elegant, quiet streets around Portman Square. The street they turned into was short, tree-lined and bordered by narrow, bow-windowed Regency houses. Sir Colin stopped at the end of the terrace where there was an archway leading to a mews behind the houses.

Eustacia studied it from the car window. 'You live here?'

'Yes. It's not too far from St Biddolph's and I've consulting-rooms in Wimpole Street.'

He got out and opened her door and they crossed the narrow pavement together. He let himself in with his key and ushered her into the narrow hall, and at the same time a tall, very thin man came up the stairs at the back.

He answered Sir Colin's cheerful greeting solemnly and then bowed to Eustacia as Sir Colin said, 'This is Grimstone, Eustacia, he runs this house on oiled wheels and his sister is my cook. Grimstone, Miss Cramp has done me the honour of promising to marry me in the very near future.'

Grimstone bowed again. 'I'm sure we are delighted to hear the news, Sir Colin and Miss Crump. My felicitations.'

Sir Colin swept Eustacia across the hall and into a charming room overlooking the street. 'Take Miss Crump's coat, will you, Grimstone, and may we have some tea? We have to go out very shortly but shall be back for dinner if Rosie can manage something. I'll be down at Turville tonight.'

'Very good, sir, I will speak to Rosie.'

When he had gone Sir Colin sat her down in a small armchair by the brisk fire, sat himself down opposite her and observed, 'Grimstone appears severe, but in fact he has a heart of gold and a very wise old head. He'll be your slave but he will never admit to it.'

'He's been with you for a long time?'

'He was with my father and mother. They lived here when my father was alive; when my mother moved to Castle Cary, Grimstone elected to stay here and run the house for me. He doesn't like the country.'

While they had their tea she looked around her. The room wasn't very large but the furniture, mostly Regency and comfortable chairs and sofas, suited it very well for there wasn't too much of it.

'I've hardly altered anything,' observed Sir Colin, almost as though he had read her thoughts. 'My father inherited this house from an aunt and it had been in her family for a very long time. I loved living here when I was a child, although I'm just as fond of the house at Turville. The best of both worlds—it hardly seems fair...'

'If you idled away your days it wouldn't be fair, but you work hard and you help people—save their lives—take away their pain.'

He said without conceit, 'I do my best; my father was a physician, so was his father, and I don't think they ever quite forgave me for taking up surgery.' He put down his cup. 'Shall we go and see this bishop and see what he can do for us?'

He took her to a nice old house in Westminster and the bishop, an old man with bright blue eyes which missed nothing, approved of her. There were certain formalities, he explained, which he would be delighted to arrange, and he could see no reason why they shouldn't marry within about a couple of weeks in Turville Church. 'And I hope I shall be invited to the wedding.'

Eustacia glanced at Sir Colin and saw his faint smile. 'I don't suppose you would marry us?' she ventured.

'My dear young lady, I hoped that you might ask that. I shall be delighted. I will get in touch with your rector, and you of course will be going to see him.'

'It will have to be tomorrow evening...'

They left presently and, as they drove back to the house, Sir Colin said, 'I'll leave you to choose the day, Eustacia. If you could let me know by the weekend I can organise a couple of days free.'

No honeymoon, she reflected, but a honeymoon would be silly in the circumstances; they were entering a kind of business partnership for the sake of the boys, and she mustn't forget that. She agreed pleasantly and later, sitting in the drawing-room drinking her sherry before dinner, she followed his lead and kept the talk impersonal.

They dined deliciously; tomato and basil soufflé, roast lamb with new potatoes and purée of broccoli and a syllabub with ginger biscuits. The white burgundy she was offered pleased her and loosened her tongue too, so that her host sat back with a glint in his eyes, encouraging her to talk.

She was taken aback when, instead of Grimstone, his sister Rosie came in with the coffee-tray. She beamed at Eustacia as she put the tray on the table. 'I'm sorry that I hadn't the time to plan a good dinner for you, seeing as how you're engaged and that. And I'm sure I wish you both very happy. I did the best I could but there weren't no time.'

'It was a delicious dinner,' said Eustacia, and she meant it. 'Those ginger biscuits—you made them yourself, of course.'

Rosie's smile became even wider. 'Indeed I did, Miss Crump. I don't allow Sir Colin to eat any of those nasty cakes and biscuits from the shops. Sawdust and sugar, I always say.'

'I'm sure you look after him beautifully, Rosie, and it really was a super dinner.'

Rosie retired, still smiling, and Sir Colin, who hadn't said a word, drank his coffee and she said uneasily, 'I've annoyed you, haven't I?'

'Now why should you say that, Eustacia? On the contrary, I have been thinking that you have the gift of instant empathy.'

'Oh, have I? I like people—well, most people.' She thought of Mrs Kennedy and hoped that next time they met the meeting would be a happier one, though she doubted it.

They drove back to Turville very shortly afterwards, to discuss their plans with her grandfather, but not before Eustacia had nipped up to the boys' room and made sure that they were sleeping. Oliver opened an eye as she peered at them both by the light of the dim night-light she thought it prudent to allow them.

'You're back? Is Uncle with you?'

She tucked him up and dropped a kiss on the top of his head. 'Yes, dear, but he has to go again after breakfast. Now go to sleep like a good boy.'

She went to bed herself shortly afterwards—the day had been full of surprises and she hadn't been given time to think about them. Once in bed, she allowed her thoughts to wander. Her grandfather and Sir Colin had been so matter-of-fact about the whole thing, she thought peevishly, as though the kind of upheaval she had experienced that morning was a perfectly normal happening—and now she came to think about it, perhaps she had been too hasty. It had all sounded so sensible when Sir Colin had suggested that they should marry, but now a hundred and one reasons why she should cry off reared their heads. An hour later, from whichever angle she looked at it, the reason for marrying Sir Colin more than cancelled out her own against. The Kennedys, she felt sure, were quite capable of doing their utmost to have the care of the boys unless Sir Colin could provide them with a stable background. And, of course, if she married him the background would be just that. They were dear children and they had been dealt a bitter blow, and Sir Colin was so obviously the right person to give them a home. She slept on the thought.

Sir Colin left after breakfast with the promise of a speedy return, and it was left to Eustacia to enlarge upon the plans for the wedding. The rest of the week was largely taken up with discussions involving the actual wedding, the prospect of school and what Eustacia was to wear. It must be white, they told her, but she drew the line at a train, six bridesmaids and a diamond tiara. 'Would a pretty hat do?' she wanted to know. 'And no bridesmaids, but I promise you that I'll wear white,'

In the quiet of her room she did anxious sums; she had saved her salary and there was a small amount in the bank. It wasn't just the wedding dress—she simply had to have a suit and some shoes and a dress—one which she could wear if by any chance someone came to dinner or they went out. It didn't seem very likely; she en-visaged a quiet future, with her living with the boys at Turville, making a home for them. That was why she was marrying Sir Colin, wasn't it?

He came home at the weekend, swept them all off to church on Sunday morning, took the boys for a walk after lunch and drove her back to London after tea. Over dinner he told her that he would be at the hospital for the next two days, going from there to his consulting-rooms and getting back for dinner in the evening. 'I'll drive you back on Wednesday evening,' he told her. 'Can you get your shopping done in that time?' He smiled his gentle smile. 'Have you enough money?'

'Oh, yes, I think so.'

'How much?'

And when she told him, 'You will have an allowance when we are married. I think it might be a good idea if I give it to you before you start your shopping.' And when she demurred, 'No, please don't argue, Eustacia. I have a number of friends and we shall have social occasions to attend together as well as the occasional weekend when we are away or entertaining guests at Turville. Buy all the clothes you will need and, if you run out of money, let me know.'

She thanked him quietly; there was no point in arguing about it for he made sense—her wardrobe was scanty, out of date and quite unsuitable for the wife of an eminent surgeon.

They didn't talk about it again. He told her that he had arranged for the wedding to take place on the day she had wanted, and there would be fifty or sixty guests coming. 'Short notice, I know, but I know most of them well enough to phone them.'

She went to bed soon after dinner and he made no attempt to keep her up. He opened the door for her and put a hand on her arm as she passed him. 'Don't worry, it will work out perfectly.'

He kissed her cheek and wished her goodnight, and she wondered if he had meant the wedding or their future together.

He had gone when she went down in the morning. She had slept peacefully in the charming room with its pastel colours and silk curtains, and it had been bliss to be roused by Rosie with early-morning tea. There was an envelope on the tray with a note from Sir Colin hoping that she had had a good night's sleep. There was a roll of notes too. Her eyes almost popped from her head when she counted them—she could never spend that in a year... The note bore a postscript: he hoped there was sufficient for her to get the wedding clothes, and he

would see that she had the same amount before the following day. 'Well,' said Eustacia, and counted the notes
again just to make sure and then, over breakfast, fell to
making a list of suitable clothes for every occasion. She
glanced down at her well-worn skirt and wondered if he
had minded her shabbiness; never by a glance had he
betrayed that fact. He was a kind man and they got on
well now that she had got to know him better. She wondered if he had been in love and decided that he had,
quite a few times probably—he might still be for all she
knew, but that was not her concern—she must remember that they were marrying for the boys' sake and
for no other reason. She shook off a sudden feeling of
sadness and applied herself once more to her list.

CHAPTER FIVE

EUSTACIA hadn't had the chance to shop with almost unlimited money in her purse for several years—her venue had been the high street stores at sale-time, and even then it had been a question as to whether it was a garment which would stand up to a good deal of wear and still remain at least on the fringe of fashion. Now, clutching what she considered to be a small fortune, she took a bus to Harrods.

She paused for an early lunch, surrounded by dress-boxes and elegant packages, the possessor of a wedding dress, a charming hat to go with it, elegant shoes she felt she would never wear again after the wedding-day, a beautifully tailored suit in a rich brown tweed, sweaters and blouses to wear with it, and two dresses which she hoped would be suitable for any minor social occasion. She scanned her list as she ate her asparagus flan and decided what to buy next. A decent raincoat and stout shoes, and, if there was any money left, a pretty dressing-gown and slippers, and even if there was any money left after that she doubted whether she would be able to carry any more parcels, even as far as a taxi.

It was teatime when she arrived back at Sir Colin's house. Grimstone must have been on the look-out for her for he opened the door as she got out of the taxi, paid the driver and carried her packages inside.

'A successful day, Miss Crump?'

'Oh, very, thank you, Grimstone, I've had a lovely time.'

'I will convey these to your room, miss, and tea will be served in the drawing-room in ten minutes' time if that is suitable to you?'

There seemed an awful lot of boxes and bags, but she resisted the desire to open them and take a look, tidied herself in a perfunctory fashion and went downstairs. Tea had been arranged on a small table before the fire; tiny sandwiches, strips of toast, little iced cakes arranged on paper-thin china, and, to keep her company, Moses and Madam Mop the cat. There was no sign of Sir Colin, so presently she went upstairs and opened the purchases. The wedding dress she hung away in the wardrobe, resisting the temptation to try it on once more. It was of very fine white wool with a satin collar and cuffs and of an exquisite cut, worth every penny of its exorbitant price. Then she took the hat out of its box; it was white mousseline and satin with a wide brim and a satin bow to trim it, not, perhaps, quite what the boys had wanted but definitely bridal. She was head and shoulders in the wardrobe arranging the shoes just so when there was a knock on the door, and she called, 'Come in.'

She backed away, expecting to see Rosie intent on drawing the curtains and turning down the bed, but Sir Colin was standing there, leaning against the door. She said, 'Oh, hello,' and then, stupidly, 'You're home.'

He smiled and agreed; he had started his day just after eight o'clock with a ward round, operated until the early afternoon, eaten a sandwich, spent an hour in Outpatients and then gone to his rooms to keep appointments with his private patients and presently, after dinner, he would go back to St Biddolph's to check on the patients he had operated upon that morning. A long, hard day and he was tired. It struck him that the sight

of Eustacia, standing there surrounded by tissue paper
and cardboard boxes, was somehow very soothing.

'Had a good day?' he asked, and when she said yes
in a shy voice, 'Then let's go down and have a drink and
you can tell me all about it.'

The evening, for Eustacia, was quite perfect. They
discussed the wedding over dinner in a matter-of-fact
manner and later, when she said goodnight, he bent to
kiss her cheek again. 'I hope to be home soon after tea
tomorrow, so buy a pretty dress and we will go out to
dinner.' He smiled down at her and then kissed her again,
and when she looked surprised, 'We should put in some
practice,' he told her blandly, 'the boys will expect it.'

There was another envelope on her tea-tray in the
morning, and this time the money was almost double
the amount she had been given on the previous day. She
counted it and wondered if she should save some of it,
but on the other hand he had told her to buy all the
clothes she needed...

She made another list and presently went back to
Harrods. A winter coat was a must, even though it was
the tail-end of winter. There were still cold days ahead
and her coat was old and very shabby—and a pretty
dress... She found a brown top-coat which went well
with the tweed of her suit, and then she began her search
for a dress. She found what she wanted—amber satin
swathed in chiffon with very full chiffon sleeves to the
elbow and a low neckline, partly concealed by a swathing
of chiffon. At the saleswoman's suggestion, she bought
an angora wrap to go over it.

There was still plenty of money; she found slippers
and a small evening-bag and took herself off to the
undies department where she spent a good deal more
money on wisps of silk and lace, to her great satisfaction. Gloves and a leather handbag took almost all

the money which was left in her purse; she collected her purchases and got into a taxi.

She had forgotten lunch although she had stopped for a cup of coffee, and, since it was three o'clock in the afternoon and Grimstone had doubtless taken it for granted that she had had a meal while she was out, she went to her room, ate all the biscuits in the tin by her bed and examined her new purchases and then put them away tidily. By that time it was after four o'clock and she went downstairs, her thoughts on a cup of tea and some of Rosie's dainty sandwiches. Sir Colin had said that he would be back after tea, and that small meal would fill in the time nicely until he came.

Grimstone was in the hall and went to open the drawing-room door for her, murmuring in his dignified way that tea would be brought at once, and shutting the door firmly behind her.

Sir Colin was sitting beside the fire with Moses beside him and Madam Mop curled up at his feet. He got up as she paused halfway across the room and said, pleasantly, 'Come and sit down. Outpatients wasn't as heavy as usual so I came home early. Have you had a good day?'

She sat down opposite him. 'Heavenly, thank you. And thank you for all that money. I—I've been very extravagant . . .!'

'Good. There's still tomorrow if you haven't finished getting all you need.'

'Well,' said Eustacia with disarming honesty, 'I've bought all I need and a lot of things I don't, but they were so exactly what I've been wanting, if you see what I mean.'

'Indeed I do. Do you like dancing? I have booked a table at Claridge's for eight o'clock.'

Eustacia beamed at him. 'Oh, how lovely—I bought a dress—I do hope it will do.'

He smiled. 'I'm quite sure it will. I look forward to seeing it. I think we might go back to Turville tomorrow evening. I've one or two patients to see in the late afternoon but I think we might get back in time for dinner there, and to see the boys before they go to bed.'

'They will be pleased. They wanted to know when we would be coming home.' She blushed. 'That is, when we would be going back to Turville.'

'I'll phone them presently. Your grandfather is all right?'

'He's so happy... You're sure, aren't you? I mean, about me and him?'

'Quite sure, Eustacia.' He put down his cup. 'I'm going to take Moses for a gentle trot and then I must do some work. Shall we meet down here a little after half-past seven?'

It was as though he had closed a door between them, very gently, but closed just the same. She said, 'Very well,' and watched him, with Moses walking sedately beside him, go out of the room. She really must remember, she reflected a little sadly, that their marriage was for the boys' sakes and personal feelings wouldn't come into it. Perhaps later on—he was an easy man to like. A small voice at the back of her head added that he would be an easy man to love too, but she refused to hear it.

Not having had lunch, she polished off the rest of the sandwiches and a slice of Rosie's walnut cake and took herself back to her room, where she sat and thought about nothing much in particular until it was time to have her bath and dress. She wanted very much to think about Sir Colin, but it might be wiser not to allow him to loom too large in her thoughts.

The dress did everything asked of it; she had a splendid figure and the satin and chiffon did it full justice. Excitement had given her pretty face a delicate colour and her hair, confined in a French pleat, framed it with its rich dark brown. She took up the wrap and little bag, slid her feet into the high-heeled slippers she had very nearly not bought because of their wicked price, and went downstairs to the drawing-room.

She was surprised to find Sir Colin already there in the subdued elegance of a dinner-jacket, and she said breathlessly, 'Oh, am I late? I'm sorry, I thought you said just after——'

'I am early, Eustacia. How delightful you look; that is a charming gown.' He studied her smilingly and she stood quietly while he did so. 'You are also beautiful— I have already told you that, haven't I?'

She said seriously, 'Yes, at St Biddolph's—but it's this dress, you know.'

'If I remember rightly, you were wrapped in a very unbecoming overall.'

'Oh, yes, well...' She could think of nothing to say and she suspected that he was amused. 'Clothes make a difference,' she added, and her eyes sparkled at the thought of her well-stocked wardrobe.

Sir Colin silently admired the sparkle. 'If you are ready, shall we go?'

As they reached the door he put out a hand to detain her. 'Before we go, I have something for you. I should have given it to you before this, but there has been no opportunity.'

He took a small velvet box from his pocket and opened it. The ring inside was a sapphire surrounded with diamonds and set in gold. 'It has been in the family for a very long time, handed down from one bride to the next.'

He picked up her left hand and slipped the ring on her finger—it fitted exactly.

Eustacia gave a gulp of delight—it was a ring any girl would be proud of. She said slowly, 'It is absolutely beautiful. Thank you very much, Sir Colin—only wouldn't you rather I had a ring that wasn't meant for a—a bride?' She was aware that she wasn't making herself clear. She must try again. 'What I mean is,' she began carefully, 'this ring must have been a token...' She paused—there were pitfalls ahead and this time he came to her rescue.

'In plain words, my dear, you feel that it isn't right to accept a ring which should be given as a token of love.'

'Now why couldn't I have put it as plainly as that?' she wanted to know.

'And another thing—do in heaven's name stop calling me Sir Colin. Colin sounds much nicer, and as for the ring, there is no one else I would wish to give it to, Eustacia.' He bent and kissed her and he took her arm. 'That having been settled, let us go.'

Perhaps it was the ring or the dress or the elegance of Claridge's, but the evening was a success. They dined superbly: mousseline of lobster, noisettes of lamb, biscuit glacé with raspberries and praline, accompanied by champagne and finally coffee, and in between they danced. Eustacia, big girl though she was, was as light on her feet as thistledown, and Sir Colin danced as he did most other things, very well indeed. They made a handsome couple and she, aware that she looked her best, allowed herself, just for once, to pretend that the future would be like this too, happy in each other's company, content and secure. It was one o'clock when they arrived at his home but she felt wide awake, wanting to prolong the evening's pleasure. She stood in the hall, hoping that he would suggest that they talked for a little while, but as he shrugged off his coat he said pleasantly, 'A delightful evening, Eustacia.' He glanced at his watch. 'I have half an hour's work to do and I shall be gone before you are down in the morning. Only I'll see you tomorrow afternoon—I thought that we might try to get to Turville in time to see the boys before they go to bed.'

He crossed the hall to his study. 'Goodnight, Eustacia, sleep well.' The smile he gave her was what she described as businesslike; the warmth of the evening had gone— perhaps it had never been there, perhaps she had imagined it. She went sadly to her room, hung the lovely dress carefully in the wardrobe, put the ring carefully back into its little box and finally got into bed.

It took her a long time to get to sleep. It was too late for her to back out of their bargain now, and she wasn't sure that she wanted to. What worried her was that perhaps Colin had had second thoughts. But he had seemed so certain that everything would be all right, and he wasn't a man to change his mind once it was made up. What had she expected, anyway?

She slept on the thought.

The boys were delighted to see them home again and Eustacia slipped back into the quiet routine as though she had never been away—only the lovely clothes hanging in the wardrobe were there to remind her. She saw very little of Sir Colin; he spent his weekends at Turville and came there once or twice in the week but never long enough for them to talk for any length of time. That week went by and the boys started school and she drove them there and back each day, missing their company although she had enough to do now, for wedding presents were arriving and she needed to keep a list so that Colin could see it when he came home. There were discussions with Samways about the reception. The caterers would come on the day before the wedding, but furniture would have to be moved then the flowers would have to be arranged.

Sir Colin came home on the evening before the wedding, apparently unmoved by the thought of getting married. He approved of the flowers, conferred with Samways about the caterers and the drinks, teased the boys and settled down to a rambling discussion about the early English poets with her grandfather. His manner towards her was exactly as it always was, and she told herself that she was silly to expect anything else.

That evening his mother arrived and so did the bishop. The wedding was to be at noon with a reception directly afterwards and, as he had told Eustacia, he intended to return to London in two days' time. 'We will have a holiday later in the year,' he'd observed, 'and I'm sorry if you are disappointed, but my lists are made out weeks in advance and I have a backlog of private patients.'

She had told him matter-of-factly that she hadn't expected to go away. 'The boys have only just started school and they're a bit unsettled, although they are happy there.'

She wore one of her pretty dresses at dinner that evening and the meal turned into quite an occasion. The boys were allowed to stay up, and since Mrs Crichton and the bishop were there too there was a good deal of animated conversation. She went with the boys when the meal was finally finished and stayed a while, pottering around until, despite their excitement, they slept. When she went back to the drawing-room she found Mrs Crichton alone.

'The men are in the library,' she observed, 'looking up something or other legal, and I'm glad, for we haven't had a chance to talk, have we?' She smiled at Eustacia.

'Come and sit down, my dear, and tell me what you think of Colin.'

Eustacia sat and did her best to answer sensibly. 'He's a very kind man and good too. He's also generous—I've never had so much money to spend on clothes in my life before, I'm not sure that it's——'

She was cut short. 'Colin is a leading figure in his profession, and besides that he is a rich man. He would expect you to dress in a manner befitting his wife. You are a very pretty girl, my dear, and I am sure that you will make him proud of you.' She shot a glance at Eustacia's doubtful face. 'I dare say you will spend most of your time here. He would prefer to live here himself, I know, but he has always come here for his weekends and any evening that he can spare. I expect you will go up to town sometimes for he has any number of friends and entertains from time to time. I hope that during the Easter holidays he will agree to the boys coming to stay with me, in which case you will be able to go to town and stay there with him. A chance to go to the theatre and do some shopping. The boys are very happy—of course they grieve for their mother and father, but they love Colin and I believe that they begin to love you too.'

'I hope so, for I'm very fond of them both; besides, it will make it all worthwhile, won't it?'

'You have no doubts? No regrets?'

Eustacia shook her head. 'Oh, no. Not any more. I did for a while, you know, but Colin is quite right, it's the boys we have to think about.'

Mrs Crichton agreed placidly.

The men came back presently and after an hour's desultory conversation Mrs Crichton went to bed, and soon after that Eustacia said her goodnights and went to the door. Sir Colin opened it and to her surprise followed her into the hall.

'Cold feet?' he asked blandly.

'Yes—haven't you?'

'No.' His voice was kind now. 'It will be all right, I promise you, Eustacia.'

'Yes, I know that. I'll do my best, Colin, truly I will.'

He put his hands on her shoulders. 'Yes, I know that too, my dear.' He smiled his kind smile. 'Goodnight.' He bent and kissed her lightly, and she started up the stairs. She looked back when she reached the curve in the staircase. He was standing there still, watching her, this large, quiet man who was so soon to be her husband. And quite right and proper too, she thought absurdly, for I love him and even if he never loves me it will be quite all right to marry him. The upsurge of excitement and delight and relief was so great that she actually took a step down again in order to tell him so, but common sense stopped her just in time. It would never do for him to know; the very fact that they were good friends and nothing more had made it easy for him to suggest that they should marry. She managed to smile at him and ran up the rest of the staircase.

Sir Colin stood where he was for a few moments. Eustacia, usually so serene and practical, had looked as though she had just had a severe shock. He must remember to ask her about it.

They were all at breakfast, although Mrs Samways protested vigorously when she saw Eustacia sitting in her usual place. 'You didn't ought to be here,' she objected. 'The bridegroom shouldn't see the bride until she goes to church.'

'I won't look at her,' promised Sir Colin, and everyone laughed. 'Although I was under the impression that the bride took hours to dress.'

'Well, I shan't. I must see to the boys first...'

'What about taking Moses for a walk?' Sir Colin glanced across the table to his mother. 'Will you and Mr Crump keep each other company while we take the bishop as far as the church?'

It wasn't the usual way for a bride and groom to behave. Mrs Samways, clearing the breakfast things, shook her head and muttered darkly and went to the window to watch the pair of them with the two boys and Moses escorting the bishop as far as the church gate.

'And them in their old clothes,' observed Mrs Samways to the empty room.

However, she had to admit a few hours later that there was no fault to find with the bridal pair. Eustacia, walking down the aisle with her grandfather, made a delightful picture; the wide-brimmed hat was a splendid foil for her dark hair and the elegant simplicity of her dress was enhanced by the double row of pearls around her neck. She had found them on her dressing-table when she had gone to her room to dress with a note from Colin, begging her to wear them. There was a bouquet for her too, cream roses and lilies of the valley, freesias in the faintest pink and orange-blossom. Sir Colin was well worth a second look too, thought his devoted housekeeper. He stood, massive and elegant in his grey morning-coat and pale grey stock, and Mrs Samways wiped a sentimental eye and exchanged eloquent glances with Rosie, who had come for the wedding with Grimstone.

Eustacia walked back down the aisle, her hand tucked under Colin's arm, smiling at the rows of faces, his family and friends, of whom she knew absolutely nothing. She had expected to feel different now that she was married, although she wasn't sure why. The calm man beside her showed no sign of overwhelming happiness—indeed, he looked as he always looked: placid, self-assured and kind. She took a quick look at his profile and thought it looked stern too, but then he glanced down at her and smiled. A friendly smile and comforting, although why she needed to be comforted was a puzzle to her. She should be riotously happy, she had married the man she loved...

Photos were taken amid a good deal of cheerful bustle and presently they were driven back to the house, heading the steady flow of guests.

The next hour or two were like a dream; Eustacia shook hands with what seemed to be an unending stream of people, forgetting names as fast as they were mentioned. It was towards the end of the line of guests that she found herself facing a girl not much older than herself and as tall as she was and as splendidly built. She was pretty too, and dressed with great elegance. 'I'm Prudence,' she said cheerfully, 'I'll introduce myself while these two men talk. Haso has known Colin for years; he stays with us when he comes over to Holland, so I hope we shall see a lot of each other...'

'Haso and Prudence ter Brons Huizinga,' said Colin, 'my very good friends and I'm sure yours as well, my dear.'

Haso offered a hand. He was a tall man, fair-haired and blue-eyed and with commanding features, but his smile was nice. 'We are so pleased that Colin has married. I think that he is a very fortunate man, although I do not need to tell him that. When he comes to Holland you must come with him and stay with us.' He looked at Colin. 'There is a seminar in May, is there not?'

They made their way into the drawing-room and Eustacia said, 'I liked her; have they been married long?'

'Nearly two years. A well-matched pair, aren't they?'

They cut the cake presently and toasts were drunk, and after a while they found the guests began to leave.

Eustacia started shaking hands all over again. All the people from the path lab had come; Miss Bennett in an awesome hat bade her a severe goodbye and observed, 'Of course it was obvious that you were quite unsuited for the job.' A remark which left Eustacia puzzled. Professor Ladbroke, on the other hand, gave her a hearty kiss, told her that she might find being married to Colin a good deal more exacting than cleaning bottles, and went on his way with a subdued roar of laughter.

As for Mr Brimshaw, she was touched when he said grumpily, 'Hope you'll be happy, Eustacia, you deserve to be.'

She thanked him, echoing the wish silently.

Prudence and Haso were among the last to leave and Colin and Eustacia accompanied them to their car, a dark grey Daimler. 'We're going back on the night ferry,' said Prudence. 'A bit of a rush, but I wouldn't have missed your wedding for the world.' She kissed Eustacia. 'I'm sure you'll both be very happy, just like us.'

Eustacia saw the tender look that Haso gave his wife and felt a pang of sorrow and a great wave of self-pity, instantly dismissed. She was Colin's wife now and all she had to do was to give him every opportunity to fall in love with her.

He showed no signs of doing so that evening though. They sat around, the bishop, Mrs Crichton, Mr Crump, Colin and herself, drinking tea and discussing the wedding until they dispersed to get ready for dinner, a meal Mrs Samways and Rosie had planned between them. Colin's best man, a professor of endocrinology from St Biddolph's, had driven back to town but would return for dinner and the party would be increased by the rector and his wife. The boys were to stay up and Eustacia urged them upstairs to wash their faces and brush their hair before going to her room to tidy herself.

Even without the hat and the bouquet the dress looked charming. She did her hair and her face and sat studying the plain gold ring under the sapphire and diamonds. At the moment she didn't feel in the least married.

They were all there in the drawing-room when she went down, drinking champagne cocktails, and the dinner which followed was a leisurely, convivial one. Rosie and Mrs Samways had excelled themselves: artichoke hearts, roast duck with ginger, followed by Cointreau mousse and a chocolate sauce and a splendid selection of cheeses. They drank champagne while the boys quaffed sparkling lemonade and then, pleasantly relaxed, they went back to the drawing-room where, after a short while, the boys said goodnight.

'I'll just go up with them,' said Eustacia, conscious of their wistful, sleepy faces as she ushered them to the door.

Colin opened it. 'Come down again, won't you?' he asked.

She gave him a quick smile. 'Of course.'

The boys were lively and still excited, but once they were in their beds they were asleep within minutes. She stood looking at them for a moment, the sight of their guileless, sleeping faces making sense of Colin and her marrying; they had lost the two people closest to them in their short lives and now they deserved some kind of recompense.

They sat around talking until late. The Samways and Grimstone and Rosie had been brought in to have a glass of champagne and to be complimented upon the dinner, and no one noticed the time after that. The rector and his wife were the first to go and after that the party broke up slowly until there was only Eustacia and Colin left.

Now, perhaps, thought Eustacia, we can sit quietly for half an hour and talk and get to know each other.

She sat down opposite Colin and Moses pottered over to have his ears gently pulled. She was glad of that for she could think of nothing to say for the moment and Colin didn't seem disposed to speak. Presently she said brightly, 'It was a very nice day, wasn't it?'

Hardly the beginning of a scintillating conversation, but the best she could do.

'Delightful. You were a beautiful bride, Eustacia— the boys were enchanted. And it was pleasant to meet friends again; normally there isn't much time... I'm glad Prudence and Haso came; she's a darling.'

'And very pretty,' commented Eustacia, determined to be an interesting companion.

'You must be very tired—don't let me keep you up. Would you like anything else before you go to bed? A drink? Tea?' He gave her an impersonal, kindly smile and she managed to smile back, although her face almost cracked doing it.

'Nothing, thank you, and I am tired; you won't mind if I go to bed?'

He was already on his feet. 'Of course not. I must dictate a couple of letters and ring my registrar, something I should have done earlier.'

She swallowed chagrin. 'Oh, that would never do,' she said, her voice high with suppressed and sudden rage. 'You shouldn't let a little thing like getting married interfere with your work.'

She marched out of the room, whisking past him at the door. She was half-way up the staircase when he caught up with her.

'Now just what did you mean by that?' he wanted to know silkily.

'Exactly what I said; but don't worry, I'll be careful never to repeat it. But that is what I think and what I shall always think, although I promise you I'll not let it show.'

She went on up the stairs and he stayed where he was. At the top she turned round and went back to him. 'I'm sorry. I'm grateful to you for all that you have done for grandfather and me—I wouldn't like you to think that I'm not. But I did mean what I said, though it's my fault; you see, I thought we could be friends, share things... I'm making a muddle of it, though—I should have realised that there's nothing personal—it's as you said, an expediency. I'll remember that and I'll do my best to be a mother to the boys. That's what you want, isn't it?'

She didn't wait for his answer but ran back to the gallery and went into her room, where she stood looking at her trembling person in the pier-glass. For a girl who had set out to attract the man she loved, she had made a poor beginning. She took the pins out of her hair with shaking fingers, unfastened the pearls and took off the sapphire ring. She had made a mistake, she should never have consented to marry Colin, she should have turned and run at the sight of him. She undressed and lay in the bath for a long time; her usual common sense had deserted her, and all she could think of was how much she loved Colin and what she was going to do about it.

The cooling water brought her back to reality. 'Nothing,' she told herself loudly, and got out of the bath. She hadn't expected to sleep, but strangely enough she did.

Breakfast was reassuringly normal in the morning; the boys didn't go to school on a Saturday and they were excited at their uncle being at home until Monday morning and full of ideas as to what they should do.

'Shall we let Eustacia choose?' suggested their uncle and smiled across the table at her, quite at his ease. Not to be outdone, she smiled back.

'Oh, may I?' She glanced out of the window. It was a surprisingly mild morning. Do you suppose we might drive out to Cliveden and go for a walk in the grounds? I went once, years ago, and I loved it—we could take Moses too.' She looked round her, rather diffidently.

'Splendid,' said Sir Colin without hesitation, 'there are some lovely woods there, I could do with stretching my legs.'

The boys echoed him and Mrs Crichton said, 'It sounds lovely, but you won't mind if I stay here and do nothing?'

Mr Crump nodded at that. 'Yesterday was delightful, but a little tiring; I too would like to remain here.'

The professor was driving the bishop back to London during the morning; they expressed envy, agreed that it sounded a delightful way to spend a morning and accepted invitations to spend a weekend later on so that they could stretch their legs too, and everyone went their various ways.

They left half an hour later, having seen the bishop and the professor on their way, and made sure that Mrs Crichton and Grandfather were comfortably settled until lunchtime, and wrestled the boys into their outdoor things.

Eustacia, determined to fulfil the role she had promised to adopt, joined in the cheerful talk, and if she laughed rather more than usual no one noticed. It wasn't a long drive to Taplow. They parked the car in the grounds of Cliveden, got their tickets and a map of the routes they could take through the woods and set off with Moses on his lead and the boys running off the path to explore. Eustacia, walking beside Colin, kept up a cheerful chatter about nothing in particular—it was more of a monologue, actually, for he had very little to say in reply. Only when she paused for breath did he say quietly, 'I'm sorry if I upset you yesterday. It wasn't my intention. We have had no time to talk, have we? Perhaps this evening...? If we could start again with the same intention we had when we first knew about my brother and his wife?'

He had stopped for a moment, standing very close to her, and she longed to tell him that she had fallen in love with him and ask what she was to do about it. But of course she couldn't. Perhaps they could grow closer to each other through the shared aim of making the boys happy and making a home for them. She looked up into his face and saw that he was tired and worried.

She put a hand on his arm. 'We'll start again,' she told him, 'and I'm sorry too; I dare say it was getting married—it's unsettling.'

He smiled then. 'That is the heart of the matter,' he agreed. 'Perhaps we should forget about being married and return to our friendly relationship, for it *was* that, wasn't it?'

She nodded. 'Oh, yes.' She wanted to say a good deal more but she didn't, and after a moment he bent and kissed her. 'To seal our everlasting friendship,' he told her, and took her arm and walked on to where they could hear the boys calling to each other.

CHAPTER SIX

MONDAY came too soon after a delightful weekend. Eustacia, conscious of her wifely status, got up early in order to breakfast with Colin. He was already at the table when she joined him, immersed in a sheaf of papers, and although he got to his feet and wished her good morning she saw at once that he would have preferred to be alone. She sat silently, drinking coffee, until he gathered up his papers and got to his feet.

'You have no need to come down early to share my breakfast,' he told her kindly. 'I'm poor company, I'm afraid. You've only had coffee, haven't you? You will be able to breakfast with the boys. I'll try and get down tomorrow evening and I'd be glad if you would come back with me—we have to see Mr Baldock and arrange for you to be made the boys' guardian.'

'Very well. How do I get back here?'

'I'll drive you back.' He laid a large hand on her shoulder and gave her an avuncular pat. 'I'll give you a ring this evening before the boys go to bed.'

Her 'very well, Colin' was uttered in what she hoped was the kind of voice a wife would use. 'I hope you have a good day; goodbye.'

His hand tightened on her shoulder for a moment and then he was gone.

The boys were full of good spirits, and she saw to their breakfast, drove them to school, assured them that she would collect them at four o'clock and drive them home, and then she went back to spend an hour with her grandfather before being led away by Mrs Samways,

who, with an eye to the fitness of things, considered that
Eustacia should inspect every cupboard in the house.

Colin phoned after tea and the boys talked for some
time before calling her to the phone. 'Uncle's coming
home tomorrow evening,' said Teddy. 'He wants to talk
to you now.'

'It's me,' said Eustacia with a sad lack of grammar.

'The boys sound very happy. You've had a good day?'

'Yes, thank you.' Her loving ear caught the note of
weariness in his voice. 'You're tired—you've had a lot
to do?'

His chuckle was reassuring. 'No more than usual, and
remember that I like doing it.'

She remembered something. 'Shall I have time to do
any shopping when I'm in London? Mrs Samways wants
some things from Fortnum and Mason...'

'We shouldn't be too long with Mr Baldock, so there
should be time enough.' He added, 'I shall be home
about six o'clock, Eustacia.'

'Oh, good.' She had no idea how delighted she
sounded.

It was nearer seven o'clock by the time he arrived the
next day, but the boys, bathed and ready for bed, had
their supper while he talked to them until Eustacia shooed
them upstairs, to tuck them up and potter quietly around
the room until they were asleep.

They drove up to London directly after breakfast,
taking the boys to school first, and they went straight
to Mr Baldock's office. Eustacia signed papers, listened
to what seemed to her to be a long-winded explanation
of their guardianship by Mr Baldock, and presently left
with Colin.

It was a fine morning even if chilly, and outside the
office she paused. 'I can walk from here, it isn't far and
it's a lovely day.'

He took her arm. 'I'm coming with you. I can park the car close by and I haven't any patients until eleven o'clock at my rooms.'

'Oh, that'll be nice.' She skipped into the car, feeling happy. It was going to be a lovely day...and not just the weather.

They strolled around Fortnum and Mason and she bought the particular brand of marmalade and the special blend of tea Mrs Samways had asked for, and when her eye caught a box of toffees she bought them too. 'Teddy has a loose tooth,' she explained to Colin, 'and it's the best way of getting it out almost painlessly.'

They were going unhurriedly to the door when they were confronted by a small, slender woman with blonde hair, very blue eyes and a pretty, rather discontented face. She was dressed in the height of fashion and Eustacia thanked heaven that she had chosen to wear the tweed suit with a silk blouse and a pert little hat, all of them in the very best of taste and very expensive in an understated way.

Colin had stopped. 'Why, Gloria, how delightful to see you.'

He sounded far too pleased, thought Eustacia. 'I was so sorry you couldn't come to our wedding.' He smiled with charm. 'This is Eustacia, my wife; my dear, this is Gloria Devlin.'

They shook hands and smiled, and disliked each other at once. Gloria stared at Eustacia with cold eyes. 'My dear, how exceedingly nice to meet you, I have wondered what you would be like. Not in the least like me, but then it wouldn't do to marry an imitation of me, would it?' She laughed and Eustacia said gently,

'I should think it would be very difficult to imitate you, Gloria.' She allowed her gaze to roam over the woman's person, at the same time allowing her eyebrows to arch very slightly and her mouth to droop in a doubtful fashion. It had the effect she had hoped for—Gloria glanced uneasily at her flamboyant outfit and, since Eustacia's eyes had come to rest on her scarlet leather boots, bent her gaze on them.

Colin stood between them, a ghost of a smile on his bland face. He said now, 'You must come and see us soon, Gloria, must she not, Eustacia? We shall be up here from time to time—dinner one evening, perhaps?'

Eustacia smiled brilliantly. 'Oh, yes, do say you will come. Colin has your phone number, of course, and I'll give you a ring.' She glanced at her watch. 'Colin, you'll be late for your patient, we must go. It *has* been nice meeting you, Gloria—goodbye.'

'What a very pretty woman,' observed Eustacia, getting into the car. 'I'm only surprised that you didn't marry her.'

'The boys didn't like her.' His reply was most unsatisfactory. 'She is an old friend.'

'So I gather,' said Eustacia coldly.

She didn't see his smile. 'Perhaps you would like to come to my rooms and have a cup of coffee while I see my patients? Miss Butt, my receptionist, and Mrs Cole the nurse were at our wedding, and they would like to see you again.'

So Gloria was a closed book, was she? mused Eustacia, agreeing with every sign of pleasure.

The rooms were on the ground floor of a large Georgian house with several brass name-plates beside its elegant front door. He ushered her inside and Miss Butt, middle-aged, neat and self-effacing, and exuding a vague sympathy which must have been balm to such of his patients who were nervous on arriving or upset on leaving, darted forward to meet them.

'Sir Colin, will you phone the hospital—your registrar? Lady Malcolm is due in five minutes.'

Colin started for the door leading to his consulting-room. 'Thank you, Miss Butt; give Lady Crichton a cup of coffee, will you? And sneak one in to me after the first patient.'

There was a little room behind the waiting-room and Miss Butt ushered Eustacia into it. There was a small table and two comfortable chairs, a minute fridge and a shelf with an electric kettle and a coffee-making machine on it. Miss Butt got cups and saucers, sugar and milk and put them on the table and found a tin of biscuits.

'This is a pleasure, Lady Crichton, Mrs Cole and I did so enjoy your wedding, and, if I say so, you made a beautiful bride. Mrs Cole will be here in a minute or two but she won't be able to stay: she attends the patients while Sir Colin examines them.'

She poured their coffee and got up again. 'There's Lady Malcolm now. I won't be a tick.'

'I expect you have a very busy life here,' said Eustacia as Miss Butt sat down again.

'Indeed I do, and Mrs Cole too. Sir Colin works too hard, but I'm sure you know that. Going from a busy morning here to operate at St Biddolph's and then flying off heaven knows where to lecture or consult or address a seminar... There is no end to it.' She beamed at Eustacia over her spectacles. 'I dare say now that he is a married man he will cut down on some of these since he will want to be at home with you.'

'And Oliver and Teddy,' said Eustacia. 'They adore him and he's very fond of them.'

'The poor little boys. What a terrible thing to happen, but how wonderful that they have a home and two people to love them.'

She got up again as Lady Malcolm was shown out by the nurse, saying, 'I'll just pop in with Sir Colin's coffee,' and as she went out Mrs Cole came in. A small, stout lady in an old-fashioned nurse's uniform and apron, a starched cap on her greying hair.

'Well, this is nice,' she declared. 'We saw you at the wedding, of course, but there were such a lot of people there—Sir Colin has so many firm friends...'

The next patient came and went and Colin put his head round the door and said, 'Come and see my consulting-room, Eustacia.'

It was a restful place, like the waiting-room, soothing greys and a gentle green with a bowl of spring flowers by the window. His desk was large and piled with papers and she imagined him sitting at it, listening patiently to whomever was sitting in the chair on the other side of it.

This was a side of him she didn't know and she suddenly wished that she did. 'May I come to St Biddolph's one day—just to see where you work? The wards and the outpatients and the operating theatre, if that's allowed.'

'Of course it's allowed, if I say so.' He gave her a thoughtful look. 'You would really like to see everything there?'

She nodded. 'Yes, please. You see, if I know where you are, I can——' She stopped; it wouldn't do to let him think that she was deeply interested in everything he did.

He smiled a little. 'It is a strange thing, but I feel as though you have been my wife for a long time...'

'Oh, why do you say that?'

He grinned, sitting on the edge of his desk, his long legs stretched out before him. 'You behave absolutely exactly as one imagines a wife would behave. You have slipped into the role very neatly, Eustacia.'

That brought her up short. Of course, to him it was a role, not the real thing. She couldn't think of the right answer to that and presently he went on, 'We're invited to drinks at St Biddolph's—the medical staff and the cream of the nursing staff. Next Saturday—I accepted for us both. I thought we might bring the boys up in the morning and stay the night.'

'They would love that.'

'And you, Eustacia? Will you love it too?'

'Oh, yes. Although I am a bit nervous about meeting your colleagues.'

'Don't be. I'm sorry I can't take you to lunch. I'm operating this afternoon. Do you want a dress for the party on Saturday? I'll drop you off wherever you want to go...'

'Oh—well, yes, perhaps I'd better get something. Will it be very formal?'

'If you mean black ties, no, but the women will be wearing short party dresses. You know what I mean?'

She nodded, remembering the few happy years she had had after she had left school and travelled with her parents. There had been parties then...

'You will need some money. I'll arrange with Harrods so that you have a charge account, but perhaps you have some other shop in mind?' He gave her a roll of notes.

'I'm costing you an awful lot,' said Eustacia guiltily.

He smiled. 'Get something pretty, you have excellent taste.' He waited while she stowed the money away. 'Shall we go?'

She elected to get out at Harrods. It was a shop which had everything and she was sure to find something she liked; besides, she could have a snack lunch there.

'I'll be home around five o'clock,' said Colin as she got out of the car.

'Will you have had tea?'

'Oh, I'll get a cup at the hospital. Have yours when you like.'

He drove away without a backward glance and she had the lowering feeling that he had already forgotten her.

She took her time looking for a dress. It was after her lunch that she found it. Coppery autumn leaves scattered over a misty grey silk, its full skirt cleverly cut so that it swirled around her as she walked, the bodice close-fitting with a simple round neckline cut low, and very full elbow-length sleeves. It took almost all the money Colin had given her and was worth every penny of it. She bore it back to the house, tried it on once more, packed it carefully into its tissue paper, and went down to have her tea. Grimstone had set it on a small table by the fire and Rosie had made some little chocolate cakes to follow the strips of buttered toast.

She eyed everything happily. 'What a lovely tea, Grimstone, and how delightful those little cakes look.'

Grimstone allowed himself the luxury of a smile. 'Rosie thought you might like them, my lady. I'm told you will be here for the weekend with the young gentlemen. If there is anything special you would like to have you have only to say.'

'I'm sure Rosie must know better than I do what the boys like to eat, but I'll come and see her presently, shall I?'

She spent half an hour in the delightful kitchen, sitting at the table with Rosie while they discussed the merits of potatoes roasted in the oven and those baked in their skins. 'I'm sure the boys will eat them if they're smothered in butter,' said Eustacia. 'How about Sir Colin?'

'Well, he likes a nice roast potato, my lady, but I could do some of each...' They settled on a menu to suit everybody and Eustacia went back to the drawing-room, reflecting that, although she had found being called 'my lady' very strange at first, now she hardly noticed it. One could get used to everything, given time, even being married to a man who didn't love one.

Colin got back just before six o'clock. 'Give me fifteen minutes to shower and change,' he begged her. 'You're ready to leave?'

The traffic was heavy, but they got back to Turville before the boys' bedtime. Eustacia took her purchases to her room, did things to her face and hair and went downstairs to find Colin playing Snakes and Ladders with the boys and her grandfather. They looked up and smiled as she went in but returned to the game immediately, so that after a minute or two she went to the kitchen to see Mrs Samways and take her the things she had wanted.

'I'll keep dinner back until Sir Colin has gone, shall I?' asked Mrs Samways. 'Pity he can't stay the night. Always on the go, he is.'

Eustacia said faintly, 'Yes, isn't he? Do wait until he is gone if you can do so without spoiling anything. The boys will still have to go to bed...'

She went back to the drawing-room and found that the game was finished and Colin was standing with his back to the fireplace, his hands in his pockets. 'Ah, there you are,' he observed cheerfully. 'I'll be off again.'

'So Mrs Samways has just told me,' said Eustacia waspishly.

'The hospital board of governors are meeting this evening and they have asked me to look in——'

'Oh, yes? Where will you dine?'

'Rosie will find something for me.' He was still infuriatingly cheerful. He bade the boys goodnight, reminded them that he would be back on Friday evening, wished Mr Crump goodnight too and went to the door, sweeping her along with him. In the hall he asked, 'You're cross—why?'

'I am not in the least cross. After all, there is no reason why I should be told of your plans.' She made the remark with a cold haughtiness which would have shrivelled a lesser man.

He actually laughed. 'Oh, I am sorry, Eustacia. I am so used to a bachelor's way of living. I promise you I'll try to remember that I'm married now. No hard feelings?'

'No,' said Eustacia, loving and hating him at the same time, wondering if it would be possible to be out of the house with the boys when he got back on Friday evening. Serve him right. What was sauce for the goose was sauce for the gander.

'Expect me on Friday evening.' He gave her an avuncular pat on the shoulder and went out to his car and drove away with a wave of the hand as he went.

Standing in the doorway, she waved back, quite unable to see him clearly through the tears she was doing her best not to shed. She wiped them away roughly; the boys would have to be put to bed and they had sharp eyes.

It was during dinner that her grandfather asked, 'What's the matter, Eustacia?'

'The matter? Nothing, Grandpa.' She smiled at him. 'I expect I'm a bit tired—it was quite a long day and I went shopping and then Colin took me to his consulting-rooms...' She enlarged upon this for some minutes and her grandparent said,

'I dare say it is as you say, my dear. It is so peaceful here after Kennington, although I dare say Colin's house is quiet enough.'

'Oh, it is, not at all like the London we lived in.' She began to tell him about the house there and presently they parted for the night.

She was still determined to be out of the house when Colin got home on Friday evening. She was being unreasonably unkind, she knew that, but she wanted to do something to make him aware of her and chance was on her side. There was a bazaar in the village in aid of the church and at the end of the afternoon there was to be a conjuror, a treat the boys didn't want to miss.

'But will it be over before Uncle gets home?' asked Oliver.

'I'm not sure, but I don't think he will mind if we're home a bit late.'

Sir Colin got back earlier than he had expected; indeed, he hadn't stopped for the usual cup of tea after his list, aware of a desire to get to Turville as quickly as possible. He had told his registrar to phone him if it was necessary, made his excuses to Theatre Sister who had a tray of tea waiting in her office, and had driven himself off.

'Well, I've never known him miss his tea,' said Sister, much aggrieved.

'He's never been married before,' observed his registrar. 'She's a beauty—you'll see her on Saturday.'

The house was quiet as Sir Colin let himself in, and the drawing-room was empty. Mr Crump was in the library enjoying a good book, which he put down as Sir Colin walked in. He said in a pleased voice, 'Ah, you are home again. A busy few days, I expect?'

Sir Colin agreed amiably. 'Where is Eustacia? And where are the boys?'

'Oh, I dare say that they will be back at any moment; there was a conjuror's show in the village hall and she took them to see it.' He added, 'A treat, since they have done well at school this week.'

Sir Colin replied vaguely. He had telephoned Eustacia on the previous evening and she hadn't said a word about the conjuror. He began to smile and Mr Crump asked, 'You are pleased that they have done well?'

'Oh, most certainly. You'll forgive me if I go to my study and do some phoning?'

He was sitting in his chair, reading a newspaper with Moses lying on his feet when they got home. He received the boys' boisterous welcome with calm good humour, observing that they appeared to have had a most entertaining evening. 'And you enjoyed yourself too, Eustacia?'

'Oh, very much,' she assured him and smiled for the boys' benefit although her eyes were cool. 'Have you been home long?'

'I was early.' His smile was placid and she reflected that it had been a waste of time planning to annoy him. She doubted very much if she would ever get the better of him, and it was mortifying to realise that he had seen though her efforts to pay him back in his own coin.

The rest of the evening passed pleasantly enough. The boys had their supper, stayed up for an extra half-hour in order to play a boisterous game of Scrabble and went to bed, in due course, nicely tired and looking forward to their weekend in London. As for Eustacia, she entered into the conversation at the dinner table and then sat in the drawing-room, knitting sweaters for the boys while the two gentlemen went away to play billiards.

'For all the world as though we'd been married for half a lifetime,' she muttered to the empty room.

She was knitting, the outward picture of contented composure, when Sir Colin and her grandfather joined her. She looked up as they went in and enquired sweetly if they had had a good game. 'Would you like coffee? I asked Mrs Samways to leave some ready...'

They declined, and after ten minutes or so she stuck her ball of wool on to the ends of the needles and got to her feet. 'Then I'll go to bed.' She flashed them a brilliant smile and made for the door.

Colin got there first and laid a hand over hers. 'Will you spare a moment? I thought we might leave about eleven o'clock, have an early lunch and take the boys to Madame Tussaud's, and then go somewhere for tea. We'll need to leave the house at half-past six for the party—can you get them to bed and dress in an hour?'

'Just about.'

He nodded. 'Good.' He bent and kissed her cheek and then opened the door. 'I am so glad that you enjoyed the conjuror,' he murmured as she went past him.

The next morning went according to plan; a foregone conclusion, reflected Eustacia—plans made by Colin went smoothly and exactly as he wished. A light lunch was enjoyed by them all at the London house and very shortly afterwards the four of them piled into a taxi and were driven to Madame Tussaud's, a highly successful outing despite the frustrated wishes of the boys to view the Chamber of Horrors. The prospect of a splendid tea made up for this and they did full justice to the meal, served with great elegance in Claridge's Hotel; sandwiches, buns and small cream cakes were polished off with the assistance of a sympathetic waiter who produced an unending supply of delicacies and orange squash.

'Did we behave well, Eustacia?' asked Oliver as they got out of the taxi and went indoors.

'You were both quite perfect,' she declared. 'I was proud of you—weren't you, Colin?'

She turned to him and found him watching her with an expression which puzzled her. She forgot it once she was engulfed in the bustle of getting the boys to their beds, arranging for them to have milk and sandwiches once they were there and then going off to dress.

She had ten minutes to spare before they needed to leave; she went along to the boys' room and found them in their beds, demanding their supper. She promised to see Rosie on her way and hurry her up, kissed them goodnight and then, since they wanted it, paraded up and down the room in the new dress, twirling round so that the skirt billowed around her.

'Oh, very nice,' said Colin from the door, 'you will be a sensation.'

She came to a sudden halt. 'Don't be absurd,' she told him severely. 'I shall be very dignified...'

'Why?' He sounded amused.

'Well, consultants are dignified, aren't they? So I imagine their wives are too.' She added slowly, 'I think I'm a little nervous of meeting them.'

'No need. You look exactly as a consultant's wife should look.' He walked towards her and deliberately added, 'Elegantly dressed, beautiful and charming. I shall be the envy of all the men there.'

She blushed charmingly but looked at him uncertainly. He was probably being kind and bolstering up her ego. She said hesitantly, 'As long as I'll do...'

For answer he turned to the boys. 'Will Eustacia do, Oliver—Teddy? Will she be the prettiest lady there?'

They shouted agreement and he said, 'You see? Unanimous. We'll tell you all about it in the morning.'

The party was being held in the large room adjoining the consultant's room, a high-ceilinged apartment used

for social occasions, meetings of hospital governors and
other solemn events, and as they went in Eustacia had
the impression that it was packed to the ceiling with
people.

She felt Colin's hand, large and reassuring, on her
arm as they made their way to where the hospital
governors and his colleagues were waiting. After that,
she began to enjoy herself. The men were plainly interested in her and their wives were kind. Presently she
found that Colin had been surrounded by a group of
older men and she was taken under the wing of the hospital secretary and passed from group to group. There
were even a few people she knew: Miss Bennett and Mr
Brimshaw and Professor Ladbroke, and in a little while
Colin joined her, introducing her to a bewildering
number of medical staff as well as the matron and several
of the senior sisters. When the medical director called
for silence, Colin took her hand and held it fast, which
was a good thing, for the medical director, elderly and
forgetful and of a sentimental turn of mind, made a long
speech about the joys of marriage and young love before
presenting them with a wedding gift. A silver rose-bowl
which Eustacia received with a shy smile and a murmured thank you. It was left to Sir Colin to reply and
anyone listening to him, she thought, would think that
he was head over heels in love and blissfully happy. Indignant colour flooded her cheeks and everyone looked
at her and smiled kindly, thinking that she was shy.

She smiled in return, while she reflected with something like dismay on a future full of pitfalls. Marrying
Colin for a sensible and good reason was one thing, but
to have to enact a loved and loving wife for the rest of
her days was suddenly unendurable, since he had shown
no desire to have a loving wife, only a surrogate mother
for his nephews.

They left soon after with enough invitations for morning coffee and dinner parties to keep them occupied for weeks to come. As they got into the car Eustacia said, 'You're very popular, aren't you, Colin?'

'I have been working at St Biddolph's for years,' he told her, as though that were sufficient answer, and then he added placidly, 'I dare say I should not have received half as many invitations if you hadn't been with me. I can see that you will be a great asset to me, Eustacia.'

She glanced at his calm profile. 'I shouldn't have thought that you needed assets.' She sounded very slightly cross.

'For some reason patients are much more at ease with their medical adviser if he is a married man.'

'What a good thing,' declared Eustacia sharply. 'I must bear that in mind.'

'Yes, do,' said Colin at his most bland.

The boys were still awake when they got back, so they said goodnight for a second time and then sat down to their dinner. 'Would you like to go out this evening?' Colin asked. 'A night-club or dancing?'

She took a mouthful of Rosie's delicious asparagus soup and thought about it. 'Unless you want to, no, thank you...'

'Oh, good. I seldom get a quiet evening at home. I can catch up on my reading, there may be something worth watching on TV, and there are several new novels you may like to dip into.'

But no conversation, thought Eustacia. 'It sounds delightful,' she said with what she hoped was suitable wifely acquiescence, and she quite missed the gleam of amusement in her husband's eye.

They went to the drawing-room and had their coffee and she chose a book and opened it, and Sir Colin, with what she imagined was a sigh of contentment, unfolded the evening paper. She had read page one and embarked on page two when the front doorbell pealed and she heard Grimstone's measured tread crossing the hall and then the murmur of voices. A moment later he opened the drawing-room door and announced, 'Miss Gloria Devlin.'

She came tripping into the room, a brilliant figure in a magenta silk trouser-suit with a black camisole top, and had begun to talk before Sir Colin had cast aside his newspaper and risen to his feet.

'My dears, I heard you were in town for the weekend and after that dreary drinks party at the hospital I knew you would be longing for a lively evening.' She paused as a youngish man came into the room. 'So Clive and I put our heads together and came round to collect you both. We can go to a night-club...' She looked at Eustacia. 'You haven't met Clive, have you? He's a scream and such good fun.'

'How delightful to see you, Gloria,' Sir Colin was at his most urbane, 'and so kind of you to think of us.' He nodded at her companion. 'Do come in and have a drink. Unfortunately we have other plans for the evening, so we must refuse your invitation, but stay for a while. Sit here, by the fire, Gloria. What will you drink?'

'Oh, my usual, vodka—you surely haven't forgotten after all these months?' She gave a little tinkling laugh and Eustacia wanted to box her ears.

Sir Colin made no answer to this but poured her drink and turned to the man. 'And you, Stevenson?'

'Whisky, thanks.'

'You haven't met my wife, I believe?' went on Sir Colin smoothly. 'Eustacia, this is Clive Stevenson, he runs a clinic for plastic surgery.' He added, 'Would you like a drink, darling?' He smiled across the room at her. 'Perhaps you had better not, since we're going out again.'

She smiled back. 'I don't want anything, thank you, dear.' She turned to Gloria. 'I didn't see you at St Biddolph's this evening.'

'Me? Go there? It's the last place that I'd set foot in. Clive heard about it from one of the doctors there—he anaesthetises for him. Clive has a huge practice making tucks and face-lifting. He alters shapes too...' She gave Eustacia's person a penetrating look, but since there was nothing wrong with it she remained silent, but Stevenson chimed in with a laugh,

'No good looking at our hostess, Gloria, she looks perfect to me.'

Eustacia gave him a look to freeze his bones and glanced at Sir Colin. His face was without expression but his mouth had become a thin line.

'You must forgive us,' he said in a voice which conveyed the fact that he had not the least interest in their forgiveness. 'We are due to leave in a very short time and I must phone to the hospital first.'

Gloria pouted. 'Oh, Colin, how dull of you to go off on your own, just the two of you—we could have had such a good time.' She cast a sly look at Eustacia. 'As we used to...'

Sir Colin took no notice of this remark and she shrugged her shoulders and got up. 'Oh, well, we might as well go and leave you to your domestic bliss.'

Eustacia got up too. 'So kind of you to call in,' she said sweetly, 'I hope you will have a pleasant evening.'

'I'm sure we shall.' Gloria's voice was just as sweet. 'Though I rather think our ideas of a pleasant evening aren't the same.' She tripped over to Sir Colin and leaned up to kiss him, then grabbed Clive's arm. He had gone over to say goodbye to Eustacia and Gloria gave him a tug. 'Come on, Clive, it's me you are taking out.' She gave another of her irritating trills of laughter. Eustacia

watched them go and stood listening to them talking to
Colin in the hall, wondering what they were saying. A
pity the door was almost closed...

Sir Colin came back presently and picked up his paper.
Eustacia addressed the back of it. 'I am sorry if it's in-
convenient to you, but I do not like your friends,' she
observed waspishly, 'at least, some of them.'

He lowered the paper and looked at her over it.
'Hardly friends—I don't care for Stevenson——'

'She kissed you...' She hadn't meant to say that and
she frowned furiously.

'I have yet to meet a man who didn't enjoy being kissed
by a pretty woman.' He spoke with maddening calm,
but his eyes beneath the heavy lids were watching her
cross face with hidden amusement.

It seemed impossible to get the better of him; there
was no answer to that. She put down her book and rose
with dignity. 'The prospect of looking at the back of
your newspaper for the rest of the evening leaves me
with no alternative but to go to bed. Goodnight, Colin.'

She sailed to the door and most unfortunately tripped
up as she reached it; he was just in time to set her on
her feet again, making no effort to let her go. 'Thank
you,' she said coldly. He smiled down at her.

'Crosspatch.' The kiss he gave her would, in the right
circumstances, have been very satisfying.

CHAPTER SEVEN

EUSTACIA lay awake for a long time; a good weep had done very little to relieve her feelings, and the evening's events were going round and round in her head until they were in such a muddle that she had no clear idea of what she was thinking about any more. She slept at last and woke in the morning with the lowering feeling that she had behaved badly. She dressed and went to see how the boys were getting on and presently they all went down to breakfast. There was no one at the table but, looking out of the window, they could see Sir Colin in his small garden. He had Moses with him and Madam Mop was sitting on the edge of a stone bird-bath, watching them. The garden was charming, ringed around by a variety of small trees and a high brick wall, with a patio outside the house, a small lawn in its centre and flower-beds bordering the narrow paths. In another week or so there would be daffodils everywhere and, later, tulips. Sir Colin was crouching over a centre bed, planting bulbs, and the boys lost no time in opening the french window and rushing out to join him.

Eustacia watched while they gave him a hand; they were talking nineteen to the dozen and getting in the way of their uncle, and she very much wanted to join them. She was feeling awkward about meeting Colin again after the previous evening; she had been insufferably rude and, not only that, his kiss had taken her by surprise, leaving her uncertain and more in love with him than ever, a state of affairs which wouldn't do at all. She was roused from her unhappy thoughts by Rosie's voice.

'Catch their deaths out there,' she said, 'and breakfast all but on the table, too.'

'I'll call them in,' said Eustacia hastily, 'but it's not cold, is it?' She turned to smile at the housekeeper.

'Well, not so's you'd notice, my lady, but there's good hot porridge waiting to line their stomachs.'

Eustacia said, 'Oh, good, Rosie,' and opened the french windows again and yelled, 'Breakfast—now, this instant!'

She watched them go in through the garden door and presently they came into the dining-room. 'Did you wash your hands?'

They chorused a yes and Sir Colin said meekly, 'I washed mine too. Good morning, Eustacia.'

Her good morning was drowned by the boys' demands to know what they were going to do all day. 'Sit down, eat your porridge and I'll tell you,' said Sir Colin. 'Church?' He cocked an eyebrow at Eustacia, who nodded without hesitation. 'St Paul's, I think, don't you? And afterwards we'll cross the river and drive and find somewhere for coffee before we come back here for lunch. How about an hour or two at the zoo before tea? And then we'll go back to Turville.'

This programme was greeted with approbation by the boys and, after they had made a hearty breakfast, Eustacia led them away to be tidied and fastened into their coats, while Sir Colin wandered off to appear in a short time suitably attired in a dark grey suit and beautifully polished shoes.

'I like that outfit,' he told Eustacia, who was waiting for him in the hall, and to her great annoyance she blushed.

The vastness and magnificence of St Paul's Cathedral did much to soothe her. She listened to Teddy's shrill voice piping up when he knew the hymns, Oliver's more assured treble and Colin's deep rumbling bass and, since it was expected of her, joined in with her own small, clear voice.

They found somewhere to have coffee after the service, and then went home to Rosie's Sunday dinner of roast beef, Yorkshire puddings, roasted potatoes and sprouts, cooked to perfection, and followed by a trifle which was sheer ambrosia.

They wasted no time in going to the zoo, and Eustacia was glad of that. There had been no opportunity to be alone with Colin, let alone talk to him; they had the boys with them all the time and when they got home they had tea together, a substantial meal of Marmite on toast, sandwiches and chocolate cake.

It was as they were on the point of leaving after this meal that Grimstone asked, 'At what time will you be back, Sir Colin? Rosie will have a meal ready for you...'

'No need,' he replied, shrugging himself into his coat. 'I'll have dinner at Turville. Go to bed if I'm not back, Grimstone, but see that I'm called at seven o'clock tomorrow morning, will you?'

Grimstone inclined his head in a dignified manner, wished them all a safe journey and they got into the Rolls and drove away.

The boys, in the back with Moses, carried on the kind of conversation normal for small boys, but Eustacia sat silent, racking her brains for a suitable topic of conversation and, since the man beside her remained silent too, presently she gave up searching for a harmless subject, so that they gained Turville with no more than the odd remark exchanged. But once in the house there was a welcome bustle and a good deal to talk about for Mr Crump wanted to know about their weekend and Mrs Samways wanted to know about the boys' supper.

That attended to, Eustacia went to her room, tidied herself and went back downstairs to warn Mrs Samways that Sir Colin would be staying for dinner.

'I thought he might, my lady. Me and Rosie, we're used to him coming and going, as it were, though I dare say now he's settled down he'll get a bit more regular in his ways, if you don't mind me saying so.'

Eustacia assured her that she didn't mind in the least. 'Though I dare say it will take a little time to adjust, Mrs Samways.'

'No doubt, my lady, but you'll attend to that, I'll be bound.'

Eustacia agreed, thinking that it would be very unlikely, and went to preside over the boys' supper and then to get them bathed and into their beds. They were tired and went willingly enough after protracted good-nights to their uncle.

Once they were settled she went along to her room and changed her clothes. There was a rather nice Paisley-patterned dress hanging in the wardrobe which hadn't been worn yet. She put it on and was pleased with the result; Colin might even notice...

They had drinks and then dined, the three of them, and the conversation was of nothing in particular; indeed, she had the suspicion that Colin was encouraging her grandfather to reminisce so that conversation between the two of them was unnecessary, and very soon after they had had coffee he declared that he had to get back. 'I've a round at eight o'clock tomorrow,' he explained, 'and a list after that, but I'll try and get down in a couple of days.'

Eustacia went out into the hall with him and stood watching him while he got into his coat.

'We're bound to get some invitations to dine,' he told her cheerfully, 'but I'll ring you each evening and we can decide what to do about them.'

'Very well. And if there are any messages for you?'

'Oh, let Grimstone know, he'll find me and pass them on.' He broke off as Samways came into the hall. 'Samways, tell Mrs Samways that dinner was excellent, will you? Lady Crichton will let her know when I'm coming down again—in a day or so, I hope.'

Samways inclined his head gravely, wished him a good journey and withdrew discreetly.

Eustacia waited until he had shut the door behind him. 'I cannot think,' she declared pettishly, 'how it is that you manage to have such willing staff at both your homes. Some of the wives I met at the party were saying that they couldn't get anyone, not even cleaning ladies.'

He ignored the pettishness and answered her seriously. 'I pay them well, I house them well, I give them due credit for work well done, just as I hope that my patients give me credit when I succeed in making them better.' He grinned suddenly. 'And I inherited Grimstone.'

She felt foolish and muttered, 'Oh, yes, so you did,' and looked away from his amused glance and raised eyebrows. She had been silly to talk like that and now she suspected that he was laughing at her.

'Take care of the boys,' he said gently, 'and take care of yourself.'

She nodded, hoping that he would kiss her, but he smiled again and opened the door and was gone.

She went to bed presently, a prey to highly imaginative doubts as to where Colin had gone and what he was doing. Gloria loomed large, set against a background of exotic night-clubs and restaurants with pink-shaded table-lamps. After all, she told herself worriedly, Colin had never actually said that he hadn't been, at some time, in love with Gloria—he might still be, although she was quite sure that now he was married he would give her up—although in this modern world, she reflected gloomily, it would be quite permissible for him to continue to be friends with the woman. From what Gloria had said, they had known each other for a long time. She went to sleep at last, having convinced herself that the pair of them were in some remote restaurant, looking into each other's eyes and breaking their hearts silently. She woke once in the night and it all came flooding back, more highly coloured then ever. 'I hate the woman,' said Eustacia angrily before she went to sleep again...

The day seemed endless; she did flowers, talked to her grandfather, discussed the meals with Mrs Samways and ferried the boys to and from school. By eight o'clock, she had given up hope of Colin telephoning.

It was almost ten o'clock when he did, and quite forgetful of her role of concordant partner she snapped, 'It's almost ten o'clock—you're late.'

Sir Colin thought of his busy day, not yet over, but all he said was, 'Is there something worrying you?' and that in the mildest of voices.

'No, but you said——'

He said smoothly, 'I am not always able to keep to an exact timetable, Eustacia.'

She said recklessly, common sense quite drowned in vivid imagination, 'I suppose you've been out to dinner with—with someone?'

Sir Colin, who had got through his day on a sandwich and a beer and a cup of tea forced upon him by his theatre sister, said equably, 'If that is what you think, my dear, who am I to deny it?' He laughed suddenly. 'You have Gloria in mind?'

Eustacia put down the receiver with a thump and burst into tears.

She felt terrible about it in the morning; she had been a fool and behaved like a silly, jealous schoolgirl, probably he would never want to see her again, she was utterly unsuitable as his wife and she had made a hash of being married to him. With a great effort she managed to behave normally towards the boys, listening to their ideas about the Easter holidays, now looming. 'It would be nice to go away on holiday,' said Teddy, 'but it might be cold at the seaside.'

She agreed that it certainly would be. 'But there are heaps of other things we can do,' she promised. 'Perhaps your uncle will be able to spare the time to take you to see your Granny.'

Teddy liked that idea. 'But perhaps we'll have to go and stay with Granny and Grandpa Kennedy,' he said worriedly. 'I don't want to.'

'I dare say you would have a lovely time——'

'Only if you and Uncle Colin are there too.'

'Well, no one has said anything about it, my dear, so we don't need to think about it, do we?'

'All right, when is Uncle Colin coming home?'

Eustacia said in an animated voice, 'Oh, he rang up last night, quite late, and he had been very busy—he didn't say.'

'I hope he'll come soon,' said Oliver, 'in time for the end-of-term concert.'

'He'll come just as soon as he can,' said Eustacia, dreading the idea and longing to see him just the same.

He came that evening, between tea and dinner, while Eustacia was sitting at the small table in the sitting-room, helping Oliver with his history and encouraging Teddy to write tidily in his copy-book. The three of them were so engrossed that they didn't hear Sir Colin's quiet entrance until his equally quiet, 'Hello, there.'

The boys flew to greet him, both talking at once, and he listened patiently to a jumble of information about school and the holidays and the last day of term, and would he be there because Oliver had to recite a poem and Teddy was singing a song with six other little boys?

Eustacia had time to look at Colin as he bent his height to the little boys' level. He was tired, and his handsome looks showed lines of fatigue, but he answered the boys' excited questions, came to the table to look at their homework and bent to drop a quick kiss on her cheek. 'Perhaps the boys could go and tell Mrs Samways that there will be one more for dinner,' he suggested placidly. 'I don't need to go back until tomorrow morning.'

They pranced off with Moses in close attendance and he sat down at the table facing Eustacia.

'You and I have to talk,' he said quietly, 'but not now. Perhaps we can present a suitable front for the sake of the boys in the meanwhile.' And as they came running back again, 'I shall certainly be here for the end of term and I heard from Mother yesterday—she would like us to spend a few days with her during the holidays. I can manage four or five days.'

Teddy had climbed on to his knee and Oliver had got on to the chair beside him. 'Your Granny and Grandpa Kennedy have asked if you would go and stay with them. I said that I would ask you. I know you don't want to go very much, but it might be fun, and Eustacia and I will drive you up and come to fetch you home, so will you go?'

They looked at him and then at Eustacia. 'Just a week?' she coaxed.

They nodded reluctantly and Sir Colin said, 'Good chaps.' Then he added, 'And when you come home we'll do something really exciting—you shall choose.'

'May we stay up and have our supper with you?' asked Teddy.

'I think that's a splendid idea, if Eustacia agrees.' He looked at her with raised eyebrows and a smile and she said at once,

'Oh, I don't see why not, but it might be a good idea if they have their baths now and get into their pyjamas and dressing-gowns so that they can pop into bed directly after dinner.' She got up. 'I'll let Mrs Samways know...' She smiled at the three of them, not quite looking Colin in the eye.

Dinner over and the boys in bed and the three of them in the drawing-room, she handed Colin several envelopes. 'These came—invitations—two for dinner and one for drinks; they're all in town. What would you like me to reply?'

'Oh, we'll accept, shall we?' He glanced at them in turn. 'The dates won't interfere with our visit to Castle Cary. I met Professor Ladbroke this morning and I told him that a couple of weeks' time would suit us—the boys will be in Yorkshire and we can stay in town if we feel like it.' He looked at Mr Crump. 'You won't mind, sir?'

'My dear Colin, I am in my seventh heaven here.'

'I'm glad.' He handed the invitations back to Eustacia. 'Will you answer them? I dare say there will be more. It might be a good opportunity to give a dinner party while the boys are in Yorkshire—in town, I think, don't you? You too, of course, sir.'

'That would be delightful, but I wouldn't wish you to feel compelled to invite me.'

'You need have no fear of that; I don't see enough of you—of any of you.'

His glance lighted upon Eustacia who, with her knitting in her lap, had been watching him. They stared at each other for a long moment before she picked up her needles and began to knit furiously.

The house came alive when he was at home, but once he had gone again in the morning it sank back into its peaceful state. Eustacia was glad when the boys were back from school in the afternoon, taking her attention so that she had little time to think.

School was to break up at the end of the week, and the evening before Sir Colin came home. He would have to go again on the Monday morning, he explained, but only for a few days and then they would all go to Castle Cary. His manner towards Eustacia was exactly as usual, placid and friendly, and she did her best to respond for the sake of the boys.

They all went along to the school in the morning, Sir Colin in one of his sober, beautifully tailored suits and Eustacia very smart in a new grey suit and a silk blouse and, since it was an occasion, a grey felt hat with a small brim turned up at one side. Before they left she was inspected by the boys, who pronounced her very nicely dressed. 'You'll be just like all the other Mums,' said Teddy, and his small lip quivered.

Eustacia flung an arm round his narrow shoulders. 'Oh, good, darling, and just look how smart your uncle looks. We both mean to be a credit to you, and I can't wait to hear you sing.'

Teddy sniffed. 'I do love you,' he whispered.

'And I love you, Teddy...'

'And do you love Oliver and Uncle Colin too?'

'Yes. That's what a family is, you see, people living together and loving each other, just like all of us.'

She kissed the upturned face and Sir Colin, who had heard every word, sighed gently.

The day was a great success; Teddy sang in his choir, Oliver recited his poem and they all watched the short play put on by the older boys before the buffet lunch. Once home again, their reports were studied and discussed and suitably rewarded with loose change from Sir Colin's pocket. 'Eustacia and I are very proud of you both,' he told them.

When Oliver asked, 'As proud as Daddy and Mummy would have been?' he answered at once.

'Just as proud, are we not, darling?'

He looked at Eustacia, who blushed because he had called her darling even though he hadn't meant it. 'Oh, rather—I've been thinking, on Monday suppose we drive over to Henley and buy the Easter eggs? We shall need to make a list—a secret list, of course.'

They had tea round the fire for the days were still chilly, and after the boys were in bed they dined and made plans for the next week or two.

'I'll be back here on Thursday,' said Sir Colin. 'We can go to Mother's on Friday and stay until the middle of the week, perhaps a little longer. The Kennedys expect the boys on the Sunday after that, we'll drive them up and have lunch on the way and go straight back home for the night so that I can check on one or two things. Shall we say Monday evening for our dinner party?' He fished in a pocket and studied the list in his hand. 'Eight guests, I thought, if you're agreeable.' He read out names: colleagues and their wives and the hospital matron to partner Mr Crump. Eustacia, who had half expected to hear Gloria's name, sighed with relief.

Sunday went too swiftly and she watched the Rolls slide round the corner of the drive with a pang of unhappiness which she shook off at once. The little boys had had enough unhappiness of their own, and it behoved her to show a cheerful face.

Surprisingly the days went by quickly, and Sir Colin was back once more and this time for a week at least. She packed happily, bade her grandfather goodbye and got into the car with the boys and Moses in the back, and with them there it was easier to be on friendly terms with Colin. There was a good deal of talk and giggling as they travelled and it would have been impossible not to have joined in the fun. They stopped in Hindon at the Lamb Inn for their lunch and, because Colin said it would be good for them to stretch their legs, they walked Moses down the village street and back again before driving on. It was a matter of half an hour later they drew up before Mrs Crichton's house in Castle Cary. Martha had been watching out for them and had the door open before they could reach it, and their welcome from Mrs Crichton was full of warmth. There was a good deal of milling around and happy chatter before Eustacia was led upstairs with the boys darting to and fro and following at their heels.

'You are in your usual room, my dears,' said Mrs Crichton. 'Eustacia, you are next door to them.' She led the way into a charming, moderately sized room over-looking the garden at the back of the house. 'The bathroom is through that door and Colin's dressing-room is beyond that. I do hope you will be comfortable. It's so delightful having you all. Are the boys happier now? Have they settled down?'

Eustacia was looking out of the window; Colin was in the garden with Moses. 'Very nearly. Oliver seems to have got over it better than Teddy, but, of course, Teddy's younger. Sometimes they wake in the night, you know...'

'And what do you do, my dear?'

'Cuddle them and let them cry if they want to, and then we talk about their mother and father and all the nice things they remember.'

Mrs Crichton nodded. 'I understand they are to go to Yorkshire next week. A pity.'

'Mrs Kennedy is anxious to have them. We're going to take them up and then fetch them again.'

'You and Colin will have a few days together—that will be very nice.'

'Oh, very,' said Eustacia, and some of the happiness she felt at the thought bubbled up into her voice so that her companion gave her a quick, thoughtful glance.

The next few days were sheer delight; Mrs Crichton was a splendid granny, mixing mild authority with a grandparent's legitimate spoiling. They all went out every day—Cheddar Gorge and the caves, Cricket St Thomas to see the animals and sample the simple amusements for the children, Glastonbury and its Tor. Mrs Crichton declined to climb its steep height but the boys, with Eustacia and Colin following more sedately, did. When they got home each afternoon Martha had a magnificent tea waiting for them and that was followed by an hour or so in the drawing-room, with Moses dozing at Colin's feet while they played Snakes and Ladders and Beat your Neighbour and the memory games. Sir Colin always won—he seemed to know exactly where the cards were. Eustacia, regrettably, was quite unable to remember where the cards were, but that was because her thoughts weren't on the game but centred on Colin sitting, large and relaxed, so close to her.

The last day of their visit came, and they bought presents for the Samways and the maids, and for Grimstone and Rosie, presented Mrs Crichton with an armful of roses and Martha with a box of chocolates, had a last walk down the high street and got into the car with the promise that they would pay another visit just as soon as it could be arranged. Half-term, as Sir Colin pointed out in his placid way, was a bare two months away, and it would be early summer. The boys brightened at the thought, hugged their grandmother once more and settled down in the car with Moses perched between them.

They were home in time for tea, and Eustacia, mindful of their trip to Yorkshire in three days' time, disappeared as soon as the meal was over to confer with Mrs Samways about washing and ironing and the clothes the boys should take with them—something which suited her very well, for she was becoming far too fond of Colin's company.

He drove himself up to the hospital the next morning, saying he would be back that evening. But five o'clock came and then six o'clock, and just as she was getting the boys ready for bed he telephoned. Something had come up, he told her; he would be delayed, and it might be better if he stayed in town for the night.

'Very well,' said Eustacia in a matter-of-fact voice which hid her disappointment, 'I'll explain to the boys.'

'And you?' enquired Sir Colin gently. 'Am I to explain to you, Eustacia?' And when she remained silent, 'Or don't you want to know why I'm staying here?'

She said primly, 'I'm sure if it is necessary for you to stay that is sufficient reason—you have no need to tell me anything you don't wish to.' Upon which unsatisfactory conversation she hung up, after wishing him goodnight in a voice straight from the deep-freeze.

The unwelcome shadow of Gloria hung over her as she prepared for bed and caused her to lose quite a lot of sleep so that she was hard put to it to be her usual cheerful self in the morning. Luckily she was fully occupied for most of the day, seeing to the boys' clothes

ready for their journey to Yorkshire, and they spent a
good deal of their time with her grandfather, but by
teatime there was nothing left to do and she was sitting
with them in the drawing-room, watching Samways
setting out the tea, when Sir Colin walked in.

He crossed the room to her chair and bent to kiss her
cheek before returning to the boys' excited welcome and
her grandfather's sober one.

Eustacia was grateful for the excited talk from the boys
so that there was no need for her to say much, which
was a good thing for she could think of nothing to say.
She had been longing for Colin to come home and, now
that he was here, she was dumb. She thought with excited pleasure of the week ahead—a whole week, the
greater part of it in London. She would have the opportunity of getting to know him, perhaps.

They had tea, had a rousing game of Scrabble with
the boys before the youngsters went off for their supper
and bed and then she went back to the drawing-room.
Sir Colin was alone.

'Can you spare half an hour?' he asked her. 'About
tomorrow—it will take about five hours to drive to
Richmond. We'll go up on the A1, I'll cut across country
to Bedford and pick it up a few miles further on from
there. The M1 would be quicker but it's very un-
interesting for the boys to be on it all day. We'll stop
for lunch on the way and get there around teatime.
Would you be too tired if we drove back that evening?
We can come back straight down the M1 and be home
by midnight. We can stop on the way for a meal.'

Eustacia agreed quietly and hoped she didn't look as
excited as she felt. He poured drinks and came and sat
down again. 'The dinner party is on Monday, isn't it?
We'll fetch your grandfather up to town in the afternoon,
and if he doesn't want to stay I'll drive him back the

same night. I dare say you might like to stay in town for a couple of days? I have a list on the Tuesday, one I can't put off, but I thought we might go to a theatre on the Wednesday if you like and drive back to Turville that evening and stay there until we fetch the boys back on Sunday.' He was watching her carefully. 'Unless there's anything else you would rather do?'

'It sounds delightful, and I shall enjoy a day's shopping.' She added silently, But not half as much as I shall enjoy being with you, my dear.

They were away before nine o'clock the next morning, stopping for coffee just before they joined the M1 and then driving fast up the motorway. They stopped in Wetherby and had lunch at the Penguin Hotel and, since the boys had grown a little silent at the idea of parting, the meal was a leisurely one with the talk centred on what they would all do when they got back home again, with a few tactful remarks about the pleasures in store for them with their grandparents.

The children had been there before with their parents, brief visits of a day or so, but they had no lasting memories of them.

'Isn't there a castle there?' asked Eustacia. 'A ruined one, I mean. Did you go there?'

Oliver nodded. 'We went twice. I liked it...'

'So did I,' said Teddy. 'Mummy and me found a little hole like a cave and we hid.' He gave a prodigious sniff and Eustacia said cheerfully,

'It sounds fun. Will you buy a postcard and write to us? There'll just be time before we come again. I'm sure your granny will help you with the address. I dare say she will have all kinds of surprises for you.'

The Kennedys lived in a Victorian redbrick house on the edge of the town; it had high iron railings and a short drive to the front door, and the curtains at its

sashed windows were a useful beige of some heavy
material. The front door was large and had coloured-
glass panels and was opened by a thin woman with an
acidulated expression who gave them a grudging good-
day and led them across the dark brown hall.

The Kennedys were waiting for them in a large, high-
ceilinged room, as brown as the hall and filled with heavy
furniture. Eustacia, snatching a quick look, thought that
everything had cost a great deal of money and was of
the very best quality even if gloomy.

They were welcomed with meticulous politeness before
Mrs Kennedy swooped upon the boys to hug and kiss
them and then burst into tears. Eustacia stole a look at
Colin's face and saw that he was angry, although he said
nothing, only when there was a chance suggesting that
the boys might like to see their rooms before they had
tea. 'Eustacia will unpack for them,' he added. 'I'm sure
that you have enough to do, Mrs Kennedy.'

Mrs Kennedy wiped her eyes with a wisp of handkerchief. 'Oh, indeed I have; the planning and shopping I
have had to do, you have no idea. The boys are in the
room at the back of the house if you'd like to take them
up...'

They were shown the way by the thin woman, who
opened a bedroom door for them and went away again
without a word and Eustacia, making the most of things,
went over to the window and said, 'Oh, look, what a
lovely view of the town, and surely that's the castle?
And what a lovely big room.'

She sounded enthusiastic but her heart sank at the
sight of the two small faces looking up at her. She sat
down on one of the beds and caught them close.
'Darlings, this time next week we'll be in the car and
Uncle Colin will be driving us all home. Don't forget to
write, and do you suppose you could send a postcard to

Grandfather Crump?' She opened her handbag. 'And here's some pocket-money; I know Uncle has given you some already, but you'll want to buy presents—don't forget Mr and Mrs Samways and Rosie and Grimstone.'

They helped her unpack and then the three of them went downstairs again.

Tea had been set on a table on Mrs Kennedy's right, and her husband and Sir Colin were sitting opposite her. Colin got up as they went in and Mrs Kennedy uttered an awkward little laugh. 'Oh, I hadn't expected Oliver and Teddy to have tea with us, but of course they shall if they like to. I'm not used to small children. Come and sit down, dears.' She looked at Eustacia. 'Perhaps you would ring the bell there by the fireplace and we'll have more cups and plates.'

The boys sat one on each side of Eustacia, balancing plates on their small, bony knees, and she was thankful that they had had a hearty lunch, for tea was a genteel meal of thin bread and butter and slices of madeira cake.

'The boys will have their supper before they go to bed,' observed Mrs Kennedy. 'I'm sure Cook has something special for them.' Eustacia hoped so too.

They said goodbye presently with a false cheerfulness on Eustacia's part and near tears on the part of the boys. Sir Colin put a great arm around their shoulders. 'Look after each other,' he begged them, 'and remember about all the things you see so that you can tell us next week.'

His goodbyes to the Kennedys were very correct and he listened with every sign of attention to Mrs Kennedy's gushing account of the pleasures in store for the boys. 'They won't want to leave us,' she cried playfully, and then said a cold goodbye to Eustacia. Her husband had very little to say; Eustacia hoped that he would let himself go a bit and be good company for the boys.

She sat very still beside Sir Colin as the Rolls slid out of the drive. She hated leaving the boys and she wanted quite badly to cry about it.

She said in a rather shaky voice, 'They're not going to like it there. I do hope their granny doesn't keep crying over them, and the house is so—so very brown.'

Sir Colin laid a large hand briefly on the hands in her lap. 'I know. I hate the idea of their being there, but we have no right to prevent them going to stay with their grandparents; they must get to know them as well as they know my mother.'

'Yes, but she loves them and they love her, you know they do.'

She sniffed dolefully, and he said comfortably, 'A week soon passes, my dear.'

They were on the A1 again and then the M1, travelling fast. At Lutterworth they stopped at the Denbigh Arms and had dinner, then they drove on. The motorway was fairly empty and they made good time; well before midnight he stopped the car outside their home and Samways, appearing silently, opened the door and offered hot drinks and sandwiches.

Sir Colin glanced at Eustacia. 'Ah, Samways, good of you to wait up. A pot of tea, I think, and one or two sandwiches. We'll be in the small sitting-room.'

Samways made his way to the kitchen where Mrs Samways was waiting, ready dressed for bed in a red woolly dressing-gown. 'Tea,' said Samways, and gave his wife an old-fashioned look. 'Mark my words, Bessie, Sir Colin's head over heels even though he may not know it. Tea—I ask you—him drinking tea at this hour of the night?'

'And very right and proper too,' said Mrs Samways, arranging sandwiches on a plate. 'It's time he was a family man.'

* * *

Sir Colin put an arm round Eustacia's shoulders. 'Tired? It has been a long day.'

'I enjoyed it, though I hated leaving the boys. Do you suppose they'll be all right?'

They sat down opposite each other with Moses in between them.

'Provided Mrs Kennedy doesn't weep all over them. I know she must miss her daughter and grieve for her, but it is hardly fair to inflict her grief upon the two small boys.'

They drank their tea, not talking much, and presently Eustacia said goodnight and took herself off to bed. 'It was a lovely day,' she told him. She would have liked to have said a great deal more than that, but the bland look upon his face stopped her just in time.

They drove up to town after lunch the next day and after they had telephoned the Kennedys. The boys were out walking, they were told, and had settled down very well.

'They slept well?' asked Eustacia.

'Of course they slept well.' Mrs Kennedy sounded quite put out and Eustacia felt it necessary to make soothing sounds by way of apology. With that they had to be content.

Grimstone admitted them, assured them that everything was in train for the dinner party and bore Mr Crump off to his room while Sir Colin disappeared into his study and Eustacia, after tidying herself and unpacking her overnight bag, went to talk to Rosie in the kitchen. They had discussed the menu at some length and now she was assured that everything was going well. The sorrel soup, the grilled trout with pepper sauce, the fillets of lamb with rosemary and thyme and the chestnut soufflé with chocolate cream were in various stages of cooking and Rosie herself would see to the dinner table.

In the meantime tea would be taken into the drawing-room whenever it was wanted.

'Oh, then now, I think, Rosie, and you and Grimstone have yours before you have to go back to the cooking.'

The guests had been bidden for eight o'clock. Eustacia, wearing a new dress—a pleasing mixture of blues and greens in soft silk—went downstairs to check the dining table and then join the men in the drawing-room.

'Nervous?' asked Sir Colin as she went in. 'You shouldn't be, you look quite delightful.'

A remark which seemed a good augury for the evening. As it was, Eustacia went to bed that night feeling pleased with herself; it had been highly successful, conversation had never flagged and she had liked her guests. Moreover Colin had been pleased with her and her grandfather proud of her. The two gentlemen had driven off to Turville after the guests had gone and she had waited up until Colin had come back. His casual, 'Still up?' rather dampened her good spirits, but she said in her usual quiet way, 'I was just going to bed. Will you be at the hospital all day tomorrow?'

'Yes, it's quite a heavy list and I've one or two private patients I must see first.'

She nodded and smiled in what she hoped was a wifely fashion. She had hoped that he might have remembered his promise to take her round the hospital one day, but obviously that wouldn't be possible. She wished him goodnight, agreeing pleasantly that if he found himself unable to get home in time for dinner she was to dine alone.

'You won't mind too much?' he wanted to know.

'Me, mind? Not at all.' She smiled charmingly as she escaped upstairs, but he didn't miss the sharp edge to her voice.

She went shopping in the morning and got home for a late lunch. She had put away her purchases and sat down with a book until teatime when the phone rang. Mrs Kennedy's voice, thick with emotion, shrilled in her ear. 'He's run away, the silly child—you should have sent a governess or someone with them, I've never——'

Eustacia cut her short, ice-cold fingers running up and down her spine. 'Teddy or Oliver? And when? Mrs Kennedy, pull yourself together and tell me plainly what has happened.'

'That is no way to speak to me... Teddy, of course— oh, some time this morning, he had been rude and I corrected him,' her voice rose, 'and Oliver slapped me— he's in his room, the naughty boy.'

'Who is looking for Teddy?'

'My husband is searching the streets. Of course the child isn't far—he can't be, probably he's just hiding.'

Eustacia choked back a rage she didn't know she possessed. 'You are to let Oliver out of that room at once, Mrs Kennedy. Tell him I'm on my way to vou and so is his uncle.' She put down the receiver since there was no point in wasting time with Mrs Kennedy, and then she dialled St Biddolph's. Sir Colin wasn't available, she was told, he was in theatre, but the porter obligingly put her through to the theatre block. A rather timid voice answered her and, when she said who she was, vouchsafed the information that Sir Colin had just started to operate and was expected to be in theatre for at least another three hours.

'The same case?' asked Eustacia.

'Yes, Lady Crichton. Do you want me to get hold of someone? I mean, I'm only a first-year student.'

'He mustn't be disturbed, but when he is finished I want you to tell him to ring his home the minute he is free, tell him it's urgent. Don't forget, will you?'

She went in search of Grimstone next and thanked heaven that he was quick to understand. 'I want a car,' she told him, and, 'When Sir Colin rings please tell him exactly what I have told you. If he wants to call the police he'll do that. Now, a car——'

'The Mini is in the garage, my lady, I'll fetch it round while you collect up your things. Which way will you go?'

'Up the M1 as far as possible.' She flew up to her room and found a coat and stuffed money into her handbag, and when she got down to the hall there was Rosie with a Thermos flask and some scones in a bag. 'No time for any sandwiches,' she explained as Eustacia got into the Mini. Eustacia glanced at her watch as she drove away. She had only one thought: to get to Richmond.

CHAPTER EIGHT

EUSTACIA concentrated on getting out of London as quickly as possible, not allowing herself to think of anything else, but once clear of the city she had time to reflect. She began to wonder if she had done the right thing. Should she have told the police? But surely Mr Kennedy would do that? And would Colin be angry with her for not letting him know immediately? On the other hand, he couldn't stop in the middle of an operation and just walk away from the patient, and it must have been major surgery if it was going to last for so long. In any case, there was no point in indulging in hindsight now; she was committed to drive to Richmond and find Teddy, and hopefully Colin, when he learned of what had happened, would know exactly what to do. 'Oh, my darling, if only you were here,' she said loudly. 'And I'll shake that awful Mrs Kennedy until her dentures rattle when I see her—shutting Oliver up. She has absolutely no idea how to be a granny.'

The Mini scooted along and thankfully the tank was full; upon reflection she decided that Colin's cars would always be ready to get into and drive. A splendid man, she thought lovingly, only she wished she knew what he was thinking sometimes behind that calm face of his. Perhaps it was as well that she didn't.

She was on the M1 now, keeping the little car at seventy but driving carefully too. She glanced at the clock and was surprised to see that it was almost six o'clock—it had been some time after half past three when Mrs Kennedy had telephoned and it would be another hour before Colin came out of theatre, and in that time she would be well on her way. If she could keep up the pace until she reached Leeds she had a good chance of getting to Richmond soon after dark. The thought cheered her and she began to think about Teddy. He might, as his grandmother seemed to think, have hidden in some nearby garden or shed, or he could have wandered into a shop... She frowned—as far as she could remember there had been no shops close to the house. At least it wasn't on a main road and the traffic along it had been light. The moment she got there she was going to question Oliver, since he was the most likely to know where Teddy had gone. A faint memory stirred at the back of her head and became all at once very clear. They had been talking about the castle at Richmond and Teddy had told her about a cave there where he and his mother had been. If he was lonely and unhappy, might he have tried to find it? It was a shot in the dark but at least it was something to start with. Possibly the police would have found him by now, in which case should she take the boys back with her? But then Colin would have telephoned... She had told Mrs Kennedy that he would drive up to Richmond, but that had been a spur of the moment remark as much to give herself comfort as Mrs Kennedy. If he were free he would have come, she was sure of that, but he had a responsibility to his patients too.

It had been a dull day and dusk was falling early, but she was nearing Leeds and there were only around seventy miles left to go. She had to slow down now for it had begun to rain from low-lying clouds, but it was no good getting impatient; she kept on steadily, watching the miles go by with what seemed like maddening slowness. When she reached the outskirts of Richmond it was nine o'clock and quite dark. She couldn't remember exactly where the Kennedys lived—she had to stop twice and ask the way, and it was with a great sigh of relief that she finally turned into the short drive and stopped before the door. There were lights on in the downstairs rooms but the curtains were drawn. She thumped the knocker and the thin woman came to the door.

Eustacia walked into the hall. 'Where is Mrs Kennedy? Is Teddy found?'

'In the dining-room.' The woman opened a door and ushered her in.

Mr and Mrs Kennedy were seated at the table, eating their supper. There was no sign of Oliver. It was no time for good manners. 'Where is Teddy? And Oliver...?'

Mr Kennedy had got to his feet but his wife remained seated. She said, 'Oliver is in bed, of course. Teddy hasn't come back yet but he can't be far away—several people have seen him during the afternoon. Mr Kennedy has been out all day looking for him—he is exhausted, and although I mustn't complain I am severely shocked.'

Eustacia let that pass. 'The police? Are they searching for Teddy?'

'We thought we would wait until the morning,' said Mr Kennedy. 'After all, they can't do much now that it is dark, and since Teddy has hidden away twice already in the garden and across the road in the house opposite, that's where he'll be now.'

'How can you sit there——?' Eustacia choked back rage and walked out of the room and upstairs to the room where the boys slept. Oliver was there, a small, wretched heap in his bed, and she went straight to him and put her arms around him. 'It's all right, love, I'm here and I'll find Teddy and I'm quite sure that your uncle will be here just as soon as he can. Have you any idea where Teddy could be?'

Oliver shook his head, and his voice was tear-sodden. 'He ran away and hid twice and Grandmother was very cross...'

'Why did he run away, darling?'

'Grandmother keeps talking about Mummy and crying and saying how we couldn't have loved her because we're happy with you and Uncle Colin. We do love her, but we love you too.'

'You can love any number of people for the whole of your life, that's the nice thing about it. So, now we know why he ran away—you were shut up, weren't you? Was that after he disappeared?'

'I tried to go after him, but you see Grandmother was so unkind to Teddy and I smacked her, so I was shut up here and then someone came and unlocked the door.'

Eustacia got off the bed. 'Now, love, I want you to be very brave and stay here and if—no—when your uncle comes tell him that I've gone to the castle. I've an idea, perhaps it's a silly one, but it's worth a try. Don't tell anyone else where I've gone.' She kissed him. 'Are you hungry?' and when he nodded, 'So am I—famished. As soon as Teddy and Uncle Colin are here we'll find something to eat.'

She tucked him into bed and slipped quietly out of the house. Apparently no one was in the least interested in her movements. She didn't take the car—it was a small town and it didn't take her long to walk to the other end and take the path to the castle, a gloomy pile against the cold night sky. She had had the wit to take the torch from the car, and she was glad of its cheerful light as she approached the ruins. Nasty ideas concerning ghostly figures, tramps and thieves on the run flitted through her head but she kept on, moving into the shadow of the ancient walls.

She hadn't the least idea where to look. She crept around, her teeth chattering with cold and fright, and finally came on to an outer wall overlooking the river below. There was a railing, but she swallowed panic and started to walk its length. Halfway along, a narrow opening led to an inner wall and then a whole series of ruined walls, and she stood there still shining her torch and calling Teddy softly by name. There was no answer and she stood irresolute, wondering what to do next, where to go. She swept the beam of her torch around her and then held it steady. A little to one side of her there was a low opening, and through it she could just glimpse a small foot clad in a red sock and a stout little shoe. Teddy.

He was asleep, the deep, sound sleep only small children enjoyed—she could have walked round blowing a trumpet and he wouldn't have stirred. But he was cold and he had been crying. She wedged herself in beside him and put a careful arm round him while she thought what to do.

She would have to wake him up and probably carry him to start with until he had warmed up a little. When she got him back to the Kennedys, should she put him to bed? And would they let her stay the night? And perhaps give her some supper? Her insides were woefully empty.

She caught her breath at a whisper of sound somewhere out there in the ruins and clutched Teddy more tightly. It could be a tramp, a desperate man hiding, a ghost—there must be hundreds in a place as old as this, she thought wildly and then gave a great gulp of relief as a voice she longed to hear said placidly, 'Hello, my dear. Oliver gave me your message.' He crouched down beside her and dropped a kiss on her cheek and laid a gentle hand on Teddy.

Eustacia sniffed away a great lump of tears in her throat. 'They said you'd be hours in theatre...didn't you operate after all?'

'Oh, yes. I flew up here.'

Her tired, grubby face broke into a wide smile. 'Oh, Colin...'

He smiled slowly. 'Yes, well—later. Let us get this young man into his bed and reassure Oliver.'

'Can't we go home?'

'In the morning, my dear. There is a good deal of talking to be done first. We must talk too, you and I.' He scooped up the sleeping Teddy. 'Can you manage? Take the torch and go ahead of us.'

Going back was easy because Colin was there. They left the dark ruins behind them and went through the quiet town until they were back at the Kennedys' home.

Mrs Kennedy met them in the hall. 'Well, where did you find him? Not far away, I'll be bound. Bring him in here——'

'He needs to go to bed at once,' said Sir Colin in a firm, detached voice which Eustacia had never heard before. 'Will you send someone up with warm milk for the boys? Are there electric blankets? No? Then hot-water bottles if you please.'

He went upstairs with the sleeping Teddy and Eustacia trailed behind. Oliver was awake, sitting on top of his bed wrapped in a blanket.

'You said Uncle Colin would come and he did,' he told Eustacia. 'Can we have supper now that Teddy's back? He must be awfully hungry.'

'He will be when he wakes up. I'll find something as soon as I can, my dear.'

Sir Colin had put Teddy on his bed and was taking off the boys' shoes. Teddy began to sit up and stir and then whimper, and Eustacia said matter-of-factly, 'Hello, there. Wake up, darling, we're all dying for our supper.'

Someone knocked on the door and the thin woman handed her a tray with two glasses of milk on it.

'Well, it's a start,' said Eustacia and gave one to Oliver before starting to undress Teddy.

There was another knock on the door; this time it was Mrs Kennedy. 'There's nothing wrong with him, is there? He ran away to annoy us, I have never been so upset——'

'Could we have something to eat?' asked Eustacia baldly.

'It's gone ten o'clock, Cook will be in her bed and Mary only stayed up to oblige me—just in case you came back, as I knew you would. Such a fuss——'

'We shall do our best not to inconvenience you, Mrs Kennedy. Eustacia and I will sleep here with the boys and leave in the morning, for that seems the best thing to do, does it not? Perhaps later, in a month or two when you feel stronger, they can pay you another visit.' Colin spoke pleasantly but Mrs Kennedy took a few steps back to the door. 'Don't worry about food, we shall be quite all right.'

When she had gone Eustacia said with a hint of peevishness, 'It may be all right for you, but the boys and I are starving—— '

'So am I. Get the boys sorted out, I'm going off to buy fish and chips.'

He was a man in a thousand, she reflected, watching his broad back disappear through the door. She had the two boys in their beds by the time he returned, carrying a large newspaper parcel and with a bottle under one arm. He sat down on Teddy's bed and portioned out the food, found two tooth-glasses in the bathroom and opened the wine. Eustacia gave a rather wild giggle. 'If you read this in a book you wouldn't believe it...'

'Who wants books?' Sir Colin handed her a glass. 'Drink up. The boys can have some too.'

She ate a chip with enormous pleasure. 'Look, what do we do? I mean, tonight? And isn't anyone going to explain anything?'

He waved a fishy hand. 'You are, for a start. Try and begin at the beginning and tell me everything.'

Between mouthfuls she gave him a brief and sensible account of what had happened. He nodded when she had finished. 'Now, you, Oliver, tell us just what went wrong.'

Oliver was sleepy, but he managed very well. Eustacia kissed him and told him what a good, brave boy he was and he fell asleep with the suddenness of a child. Teddy, awake now and eating his supper with gusto, was rather more difficult to understand but presently Sir Colin said, 'I think I have enough now. I'm going downstairs to talk to Mr Kennedy.' He put a hand on Eustacia's shoulder. 'I'll be back.'

Teddy was asleep before she had tidied away the fishy newspaper. She perched on his bed, leaning her head against the headboard, and since she was tired out she closed her eyes.

It was almost an hour later when Sir Colin returned. He stood looking down at Eustacia, dead to the world, her head lolling sideways against the bedhead, her pretty mouth half open. He put out a hand and shook her gently awake and she shot upright at once, letting out a protest at a stiff neck and a stiff shoulder.

'Sorry,' said Sir Colin, 'but you can't sleep like that all night. I've had a talk with Mr Kennedy; he agrees with me that perhaps the best thing is for us to take the boys home in the morning.' His voice was dry and she wondered what had passed between the two men. 'I suggested that we might all come up again later in the year,' and at the look on her face, 'Yes, I know, but we have to try again. In the meantime that sour-faced woman has been prevailed upon to make up the beds in a guest room. I'll sleep there with Oliver, you stay here with Teddy.'

'Yes, but I haven't anything with me—no toothbrush, or soap or nightie...'

He brushed this protest to one side. 'There will be soap in the bathroom, you can clean your teeth with the children's toothpaste and your finger and you don't need a nightie...' He bent down and kissed her cheek, a light, comforting kiss. 'Get to bed, my dear, you've had a worrying time. You'll feel better in the morning and we'll all be laughing about it.'

He scooped up Oliver and went away without another word, leaving her to undress slowly, and after a sketchy wash she got thankfully into Oliver's bed, intent on sorting out her muddled thoughts. She was asleep within a couple of minutes.

She could have slept the clock round, but Teddy woke at around six o'clock and promptly burst into tears. She got into bed with him and cuddled him close. 'She said we didn't love Mummy any more, she said we'd forgotten her and Daddy, but we haven't, and she smacked me and Oliver tried to explain and she took him away so I ran out of the house... I went to the castle...'

'Yes, darling, I know. I guessed you would go there and that's why I came to find you, and Uncle Colin brought us both back here.'

'He's here, Uncle? May we go home?'

'As soon as we've had breakfast. Now, will you go to sleep for a little while? I'll be here; I'm going to get dressed presently and then you shall dress too.'

Teddy slept then and in a little while she got up, swathed herself in the coverlet off Oliver's bed and went in search of a bathroom. The house was quiet and she ran the bath stealthily, did the best she could with her teeth and, feeling guilty, dried herself on a splendid towel which she rather thought was there on display rather than for use. Wrapped once more in the coverlet, she stole back to the bedroom, dressed and did her face and hair and, since it was well after seven o'clock, wakened Teddy.

Oliver and Sir Colin were in the bathroom, Oliver in the bath and his uncle at the washbasin, shaving himself. Eustacia said good morning, urged Oliver to get out to substitute Teddy in the bath, then wrapped Oliver up in the towel, now very damp, and asked, 'Where did you get that razor?'

'From my bag. You're up early.'

'I've been up since before seven o'clock—I had a bath. Isn't there another towel? This one's sopping.' She rubbed Oliver briskly before turning her attention to Teddy, reflecting that it was all so extraordinary, like *Alice in Wonderland*, and yet she didn't feel that everything was unusual, just quite normal.

She got Teddy out of the bath and rubbed him as dry as she could and Sir Colin observed, 'Do I have to dry myself on that towel? You'd better wring it out first.' He let the water out of the bath and turned on the hot tap, sitting on the side of the bath in his trousers and nothing else, quite at ease. Eustacia caught his eye and began to laugh.

'It just isn't true,' she gurgled, 'I mean, things like this just don't happen.' She put toothpaste on the children's toothbrushes and stayed sitting on the side of the bath beside Colin. 'How will you get home?'

'In the Mini, of course.'

'Four of us and the luggage?'

'Why ever not? It will be a trifle cramped, but I don't suppose the boys will mind.' He turned off the tap and she got off the bath, collected the boys and marched them off to get dressed. They were in high spirits, and presently when Sir Colin joined them, looking as well turned out as he always did even though there were tired lines in his handsome face, they all trooped downstairs. Mr Kennedy came into the hall as they reached it.

His good morning was stiff. 'Our housekeeper has very kindly risen early and has prepared your breakfast.' He looked at the two boys. 'I'm afraid that your grandmother is so upset by your behaviour that she is forced to remain in bed; she is a very sensitive woman and the shock has been great.'

Eustacia had her mouth open to ask what shock; Colin's firm hand, pressing her shoulder gently, stopped her in time.

'I think we have all had a shock,' observed Sir Colin in what she privately called his consultant's voice, and just for a moment Mr Kennedy looked embarrassed. She wondered what Colin had said on the previous evening.

They went into the dining-room, which was brown like all the other rooms, and heavily furnished, sparing no expense, with dark oak. The table had been laid and they sat down to boiled eggs, rather weak tea and toast. The sour-faced woman was doubtless glad to see them go, but she wasn't going to speed them on their way with bacon and eggs.

The boys bade their grandfather a polite goodbye and he shook their small hands, observing that he hoped that the next time they met it might be in happier circumstances. 'Your grandmother is going to take some time to recover...'

Eustacia went very red in the face with rage—her wish to comment upon this was great, but she had once more encountered a glance from Colin. It was a speaking glance and she closed her mouth firmly and choked back the words she had wished to utter. It was a relief to get outside and get the boys settled in the back of the Mini while Colin saw to their luggage. Mr Kennedy stood in his doorway, making sure that they were going, she thought, and an upstairs curtain twitched. Mrs Kennedy was making sure too.

She got into the car and Colin got in beside her.

'Rather a tight fit.' he said. 'Fortunately we're all on speaking terms.' A remark which made the boys laugh their heads off, but they waved obediently to their grandfather as they drove away and Eustacia had a pang of pity for him; Mrs Kennedy wasn't the easiest of wives to live with.

'I hope I never get like that,' she said, speaking her thoughts aloud.

'You'll not get the chance,' said Colin, uncannily reading her mind. 'Have you enough room?'

She said yes happily, although his vast person had overflowed on to her. She would get cramped before long but she really didn't mind. She turned her head to look at the boys. They beamed back at her and Oliver said, 'That was a beastly breakfast—we're hungry.'

'We'll stop at the service station at Ferrybridge before we get on to the M1.' Sir Colin glanced at Eustacia. 'Comfy?'

She nodded. 'It's fun, isn't it? I shall have very hot coffee and hot buttered toast.' She sighed. 'There's such a lot to explain it's hard to know where to begin.'

'Time enough when we get home,' he said comfortably. 'Let's have a day out.'

They were on the A1 now, and she had to admire the way he handled the car, keeping up a steady pace, taking advantage of any gap in the stream of early-morning traffic. The boys kept up a constant stream of talk and she hardly noticed the miles passing until she was aware of him slowing into the service station and parking the car.

The Little Chef was half full, warm and welcoming. They sat round the table, contentedly drinking their coffee and orange juice and eating hot buttered toast, and presently Sir Colin got up. 'I'm going to telephone your grandfather,' he told Eustacia, 'and Samways and Grimstone. We'll go back to the town house this evening and go on to Turville in the morning.'

Eustacia, who would happily have spent the rest of her life in a high-rise flat with him, nodded happily.

The boys had recovered completely. 'We knew you'd come,' sighed Oliver, 'only Teddy couldn't wait...'

'That's all right, love, we quite understand,' said Eustacia, 'and you see how quickly Uncle can get to you when you need him. I should never have thought of hiring a plane.'

'That's because you're a girl,' said Oliver. 'Did you mind driving the Mini all by yourself?'

His uncle had sat down again and passed his cup for more coffee. 'I dare say she minded very much, but she was anxious to get to you. When you have to do something important you don't think about anything else.' He smiled at her. 'We shall have to think of something nice to do by way of a thank you.'

'A day at Cricket St Thomas,' said Teddy eagerly, 'you'd like that, wouldn't you, Eustacia?'

'Or Longleat with the lions,' suggested Oliver.

Sir Colin was looking at Eustacia intently. 'That sounds splendid,' he observed, and unusually for him he hadn't heard a word the boys had said. Nor had Eustacia—she was far too busy trying to look nonchalant even while the colour flooded her face. There was something in his look which had set her heart thundering against her ribs in a most unsettling manner.

They packed themselves back into the Mini presently and drove on.

'Since we're having a day out we might as well have lunch somewhere,' observed Sir Colin, a suggestion with which they all agreed enthusiastically.

They stopped in Madingley, a charming little village of thatched cottages not far from Cambridge. The restaurant was housed in an oak-panelled and beamed cottage and the food was England's best—steak and kidney pie, vegetables from the garden and apple tart and cream for a pudding. Over a large pot of coffee Eustacia said, 'That was a gorgeous meal—what a lovely day we are having.'

She had addressed the boys but she was conscious of Colin's eyes on her.

'We must do this more often,' observed Sir Colin. 'Supposing we drive over to Castle Cary and see Granny—we'll go to Turville tomorrow and go the day after, just for lunch and tea. How would you two like to have her to stay for a week? I'm going over to Holland in two weeks' time and I thought I'd take Eustacia with me. We can stay with friends and she can see something of the country while I'm lecturing.'

The boys chorused their approval and Eustacia said primly, 'If that is an invitation, yes, I shall enjoy going to Holland.'

They were getting into the car again and Colin turned from fastening the seatbelts. 'Haso and Prudence are looking forward to seeing you again, and I promised I'd bring you with me next time I went to Holland.'

A remark which effectively quenched any ideas she might have had about him wanting the pleasure of her company.

A dignified Grimstone was waiting for them when they reached London. And for once he was smiling broadly. 'There's tea ready for you,' he told them. 'Rosie's been cooking and baking...' His elderly face creased suddenly. 'A nasty shock it was, to be sure.'

Eustacia took his hand. 'Grimstone, you have no idea how lovely it is to be home again to such a welcome. We can't wait for Rosie's tea...'

She led the excited boys up to their room, tidied them up and sent them downstairs, then went along to her own room. She looked awful, she decided, examining her face in the looking-glass—no wonder Colin hadn't had much to say to her; her face was pale with worry and lack of sleep, and her hair needed attention. She washed her face and put on make-up again and brushed her hair and then, suddenly impatient, went downstairs.

Sir Colin came in from the garden with Moses as she went into the drawing-room and thought that she had never looked so beautiful...

They ate a splendid tea with Moses, pressed against Sir Colin's leg, gobbling up odds and ends of cake and sandwiches, and Madam Mop enjoying a saucer of milk under the table. By common consent they didn't talk about Yorkshire; Sir Colin had telephoned Mr Crump and told him what had happened with the promise that they would all return to Turville in the morning and, since the boys were tired now, Eustacia got them ready for bed and then sat them down to their supper. She was tired herself; once they had had dinner, she would go to bed. Colin was already immersed in the various letters and messages that had arrived for him; he wasn't likely to miss her.

The boys tucked up and already half asleep, she had a shower and changed into a dress and went downstairs to find that Colin had changed too. He put down the letter he was reading and fetched her a drink before sitting down by the log fire.

'There hasn't been the time or the opportunity to tell you how grateful I am to you for your part in this unfortunate incident. You must be tired and quite worn out with the worry of the whole thing. Do you feel you can tell me about it? Mr Kennedy wasn't very forthcoming yesterday evening; according to him, Teddy had been a little monster and Oliver not much better. I don't believe that, of course...'

Eustacia took a very large sip of sherry. 'They didn't have their meals with Mr and Mrs Kennedy; they had to have them in the kitchen, and each morning Mr Kennedy took them for a walk and then they went back to spend half an hour with their grandmother, who talked about their mother all the time, telling them that they must never forget that she was dead... How could she?' Eustacia polished off the sherry and set the empty glass down on the table beside her chair. Sir Colin got up and filled it again without a word and she went on. 'Of course they won't forget their mother and father and they'll go on loving them, but they can be happy too—how could she be so unkind, loading them down with her own grief? And why can't she love them? As your mother does...she's a wonderful granny.'

Eustacia drank the sherry at one go and sat back, a little bemused from the two glasses one on top of the other. Sir Colin watched her with hidden amusement. 'Indeed she is. Tell me, Eustacia, will you enjoy coming to Holland with me?'

'Oh, yes, only don't you think I should stay with the boys?'

'No. My mother and your grandfather will enjoy being in charge. I phoned her just now, and she's delighted with the idea. She is also looking forward to seeing us all tomorrow. Have the boys all they need for school next term? Do you want to bring them up to town to buy things? They're due back on Thursday next week, aren't they? I've a list on the following day—you said you wanted to see round St Biddolph's, so you can visit the wards while I'm in theatre.'

'Oh, may I?' She sat up, happy that he had remembered after all. 'And may I go into the operating theatre so that I know where you work?'

'No. You can look through the door but no more than that. Here is Grimstone to tell us that dinner is ready.'

Very soon after their coffee she pleaded tiredness and he showed a disappointing lack of desire to keep her from her bed. She wished him goodnight in a chilly voice and cried herself to sleep.

In the morning she took herself to task—she was allowing her dreams to cloud reality and she would have to stop. She was brisk and chatty at breakfast so that Sir Colin glanced at her once or twice in a thoughtful fashion; he had never known her any more than quiet and matter-of-fact with an occasional flash of temper. But this wasn't temper, he decided, it was an act she was, for some reason best known to herself, putting on for his benefit.

He sighed, for once unsure of himself.

The visit to Castle Cary filled the next day most successfully; the boys, once they were there, had a great deal to tell their grandmother and she listened carefully before summoning Martha. 'Will you take the boys across the street and let them choose some sweets?' She handed over some money. 'And they might like to buy a comic each.'

When they had gone she settled back in her chair. 'Now let me hear the whole story,' she begged. Sir Colin told her, with Eustacia sitting quietly, her hands in her lap, saying nothing at all.

'Very unpleasant,' commented his mother finally. 'Poor children. It was splendid of you to go after them, Eustacia, and to find Teddy.'

Eustacia spoke then. 'With hindsight, I can think of lots of ways of getting them back. It would have been just as quick to have waited for Colin to finish in the theatre; he got there almost as soon as I did.'

'Just as quick, but without heart. You knew he would follow you?'

'Oh, of course.' Eustacia smiled at Mrs Crichton and the older lady nodded and smiled too.

'Just so.'

They left soon after tea, racing smoothly back to Turville, and Eustacia allowed her mind to brood over the evening ahead. Grandfather would be there, which would make it easier to ignore the invisible barrier which had reared itself between her and Colin. She tried to think how it had happened, but she couldn't put a finger on the exact moment when she'd realised that it was there. Had she said something, she wondered, or far worse, had she allowed her feelings to show?

She was aware of it during the evening; Colin was friendly and perfectly willing to talk, but only about things which had nothing to do with them personally, and so it was until he went back to London on Monday, reminding her laconically that he would be at her disposal on Friday. 'I shall start my list at eleven o'clock—I'll come for you about half-past nine, if you can be ready by then?'

'Of course I can,' said Eustacia loftily. 'The boys have to go to school at half-past eight.'

They parted coolly, although Eustacia didn't remain cool for long; Gloria telephoned during the day, intent on seeing Colin. 'That Grimstone of his says he doesn't know where he is—I suppose he's there with you?' complained Gloria.

'No, he isn't. Probably he's operating at another hospital if he's not at St Biddolph's. Can I give him a message?'

Gloria chuckled. 'You sound too good to be true! Don't worry, I'll find him.' There was a little pause. 'I always do.'

Eustacia was ready and waiting when Colin arrived on Friday morning. She had dressed with care: a leaf-brown suit, a silk blouse the colour of clotted cream and simple but perfect gloves, shoes and handbag. She thought for a long time about a hat, and in the end she settled for a supple, small-brimmed felt, worn quite straight. It gave her dignity, or she hoped it did.

Colin wished her good morning pleasantly, took in her appearance with one swift glance, remarking that she looked just the thing, and swept her into the car. 'No time to waste,' he pointed out as he called goodbye to Mr Crump, who had come to wave them off.

'Which reminds me,' said Eustacia with icy sweetness. 'Your friend Gloria telephoned yesterday. She assured me that she would find you. I hope she did.'

'Do you really?' He sounded interested and amused. 'I must disappoint you. What did she want?'

'You,' said Eustacia waspishly.

He said nothing until he came to a lay-by, where he stopped the car and turned to look at her. 'You have allowed your imagination to cloud your good sense,' he told her calmly. 'I have taken Gloria out once or twice but no more than other women of my acquaintance— that was in my bachelor days and a perfectly normal thing to do, you must allow. I am not in love with her, nor have I ever been. Satisfied?'

She wanted to say no, but she said yes instead and they drove on, she a prey to unhappy thoughts, he apparently perfectly at ease.

As they entered the hospital he took her arm. He was a rather grave, well-dressed man, self-assured without being pompous about it; she couldn't fail to see the deferential manner with which he was greeted as they made their way to the theatre block. They went through the swing-doors and he stopped for a moment, looking down at her. 'You were in a bunched-up pinny,' he observed, 'you were very earnest and I suspect a little scared. You were beautiful, Eustacia, just as you are now.'

She gaped up at him, her eyes wide. 'Well——' she began and was interrupted by Sister's approach.

'There you are, sir,' said that lady briskly, 'with your lady wife too. Shall we have a cup of coffee before you start your list? I've got Staff Nurse Pimm to take Lady Crichton round the hospital. If you haven't finished shall she go to the consultant's room or come back here?'

'Oh, here, I think, Sister.'

She nodded. 'They've slipped in that case who wasn't fit for surgery yesterday—you might be a little later than you expect.'

'That can't be helped, can it?' he said pleasantly as they wedged themselves into Sister's office to drink Nescafé and eat rich tea biscuits and talk trivialities.

Presently a head appeared round the door to utter the words, 'Your patient's here, sir,' and Sir Colin got up.

'I'll see you presently, darling,' he said and followed Sister out and away through another door, leaving Eustacia in the care of a small, plump girl who beamed at her widely and asked where she would like to start.

The morning went swiftly; Eustacia poked her pretty nose into one ward after another, visited the canteen, the hospital kitchens, spent a long time in the children's ward, was introduced to a great many people who appeared to know all about her and was finally led back to Sister's office. 'It's only an implant,' said her guide, 'Sir Colin won't be long now. You don't mind if I go? It's been nice...' She beamed once more.

'Thank you very much, you've been wonderful, I've really enjoyed it,' said Eustacia. And she had, as she could imagine Colin at work now.

He came ten minutes later, in rubber boots and his theatre garb, his mask pulled down under his chin, a cotton cap on his head. 'Hello, been waiting long?'

'No. I had a lovely time. Have you finished?'

'Yes. Sister and my registrar will be along in a moment and we'll all drink tea. I'll need to take a look at my patients and then we'll go.' He glanced at the clock on the wall. 'I've a couple of patients to see at two o'clock—we'll have time for lunch first.'

That night, getting into bed, she reflected that it had been a lovely day. She was, she had discovered, slightly in awe of him, but she loved him too. She would have to try very hard to be the kind of wife he expected: well dressed and pleasant to all the people he worked with, a good hostess to his friends, and, above all and most important, take care of the boys. He had married her for that, hadn't he? she reminded herself.

He came to Turville for the weekend and they all went walking and spent a good deal of each day in the garden. There was a gardener but there was always a lot to do—weeds to pull and things to plant. Monday came too soon but she consoled herself with the knowledge that he would be back on Wednesday and they would be going over to Holland on the Thursday night ferry. 'And I'll drive down on Tuesday and fetch Mother,' he told her as he was getting ready to leave after breakfast. 'I'll stay here for the night.'

He bade the boys goodbye, dropped a kiss on to her cheek and drove himself off.

'You look sad,' said Teddy, and Oliver said,

'Well, of course she does, silly, Uncle Colin's gone and they like to be together like mothers and fathers do. Don't you, Eustacia?'

'Yes, oh, yes,' said Eustacia and sniffed down threatening tears.

CHAPTER NINE

EUSTACIA had plenty to occupy her after Colin left. Mrs Samways wanted advice as to which room Mrs Crichton should occupy, and there was a serious discussion as to the meals to be cooked and eaten while Eustacia and Colin were away. Then there was her packing to think of; Colin had said nothing about taking her out, and she supposed that he would be occupied the whole day and probably wouldn't be anxious to go out in the evening, but for all she knew Haso and Prudence might have quite a busy social life. She added a couple of dresses suitable for the evening and, just to be on the safe side, a black chiffon skirt and a glamorous top to go with it. That done, she turned her attention to the boys' cupboards, making sure that there was enough of everything until she got back. She strolled in the garden with her grandfather after lunch and presently fetched the boys from school. She felt restless and unhappy, and when Colin rang up later that evening she had a job not to beg him to come home, even if it was only for an hour or so. She was glad that she hadn't given way to anything so silly, for he was at his most casual, and after a minute or two she handed the phone to the boys.

The next day was better—after all, Colin would be coming home that evening. She busied herself arranging flowers, shopping in the village for Mrs Samways and attending a meeting of the church council. She felt rather at sea doing this but it was something that she could do for Colin, who wasn't always free to attend. She listened to plans for new hassocks, the church bazaar, the possibility of getting more people to sing in the choir and whether the steeple would hold out until there was money to repair it. She had plenty of good sense, and the other members of the council, all a good deal older than she, were kind and friendly. She offered to provide the material for the hassocks and went back home in time to fetch the boys from school.

Sir Colin arrived about eight o'clock with his mother, greeted Eustacia in his usual calm manner, handed Mrs Crichton over to her with the remark that they hadn't kept dinner waiting for too long, and went upstairs to say goodnight to the boys.

Eustacia led Mrs Crichton up to her room. 'I do hope you'll be comfortable,' she said, 'and it is so very kind of you to look after the boys. You will find Grandfather a great help; he plays chess with them and keeps an eye on their homework.'

'We shall manage very well, my dear,' said Mrs Crichton comfortably. 'You and Colin deserve a week together. I know he will be busy during the day but you will have your evenings free.'

'Oh, yes,' agreed Eustacia brightly. 'I dare say we shall go out quite a lot.' A remark made for the benefit of her mother-in-law. She had no idea what plans Colin had made, and he certainly hadn't told her about them.

They went back downstairs presently and she was able to tell him about the church council. 'I promised to get the material for the hassocks,' she finished, 'I hope that was the right thing to do...'

'Oh, undoubtedly.' He turned to his mother. 'You see what an invaluable partner I have found myself!' he remarked. He spoke pleasantly, but Eustacia found herself blushing, wondering if she had sounded boastful.

Mrs Crichton gave her a quick glance and saw the blush. 'More than a partner,' she said, 'someone to love the boys and someone to come home to each evening.'

Only he doesn't, thought Eustacia, smiling brightly.

Sir Colin went back to London directly after breakfast the next morning, and after taking the boys to school Eustacia sat down with his mother and discussed the following week.

'I'll keep to your routine, my dear, as far as possible, and your grandfather will put me right if I slip up. Is Colin lecturing every day or will you be able to spend some time together?'

'I'm not sure...'

'He works too hard,' said his mother. 'You cannot imagine how delighted I was when you married, my dear, I was beginning to think that he would remain single for the rest of his days. But now he has another interest in life and later, when you have a family, he will discover that life isn't all work.'

Eustacia refilled their coffee-cups. 'For what reason did he receive his knighthood?' she asked, and missed Mrs Crichton's surprised look.

'He hates to talk about it. For outstanding work in the field of surgery. Two—three years ago now.'

'You must be very proud of him,' said Eustacia.

'Indeed I am, my dear. He is a good son and I have no doubt that he will be a good husband and father. His dear father was, and he is fond of children.'

'Yes,' said Eustacia faintly, 'he's marvellous with Oliver and Teddy.'

Sir Colin came home late that evening. He looked tired, as well he might, but he was as placid as usual, answering the boys' questions with patience before Eustacia hurried them off to bed.

'We shall miss you and Uncle,' said Teddy, 'but you are coming back, aren't you?'

'Of course, darling. And you're going to have a lovely time with Granny and Grandfather Crump. What shall we bring you back from Holland?'

They slept at once, for they had been allowed to stay up to say goodnight to their uncle, and Eustacia went back downstairs, to spend the rest of the evening taking part in the pleasant talk and stealing glances at Colin from time to time, until he looked up and held her gaze without smiling.

She saw little of him the next day; although he didn't go up to the hospital he went to his study and spent a good deal of time on the telephone and dictating letters. Eustacia strolled round the gardens with Mrs Crichton and her grandfather, to all appearances a contented young woman with no cares, while all the while she was wondering why Colin was avoiding her. He had taken the boys to school and had said that he would fetch them that afternoon and, with the excuse of the pressure of work, had shut himself in his study. It didn't augur well for their trip to Holland.

They were sailing from Harwich and left in the early evening amid a chorus of cheerful goodbyes and hand-waving. Eustacia, in a jersey outfit of taupe and looking her best, got into the car beside Colin and wondered just what the next week would bring. Sir Colin, having emerged from his study the epitome of the well-dressed man, appeared as placid as usual; if he was anticipating a pleasurable few days ahead of him, there was no sign of it. He could at least pretend that he's going to enjoy himself, she reflected peevishly, and then went pink when he observed, 'I'm looking forward to this week; there should be some time between lectures when we can go sightseeing.'

She mumbled something and he cast a quick look at her. 'I'm sure that Haso and Prudence will have plans for our entertainment.'

The Rolls swallowed the miles in a well-bred manner and they were on board with half an hour to spare. 'Too soon for bed,' Colin said. 'I'll collect you from your cabin in ten minutes and we'll have a drink before we sail.'

The ship was full; they sat in the bar surrounded by a cheerful crowd of passengers which, as far as Eustacia was concerned, was all to the good. Conversation of an intimate nature was out of the question—not that Sir Colin gave any sign that he had that in mind, which puzzled her, for he had said several times that they needed to have a talk together.

She went to her cabin as soon as the ship sailed and slept soundly until she was called with tea and toast just after six o'clock. She got up and dressed and left her cabin, and found Colin waiting for her.

'Would you like breakfast before we go ashore,' he asked, 'or shall we have it as we go?'

'Oh, as we go, please. Is it far?'

'About two hundred and fifty kilometres—around a hundred and ninety miles. We shall be there by lunchtime.'

They reached Kollumwoude, the village near Leeuwarden where Haso and Prudence lived, shortly before noon, having stopped on the way and eaten a delicious breakfast of rolls and butter and slices of cheese and drunk their fill of coffee. It had been a delightful drive too; Colin knew the country well and was perfectly willing to answer Eustacia's questions. The country had changed now that they were in Friesland, and she exclaimed with delight as they drove through the village and turned in through high wrought-iron gates and

stopped before a three-storeyed house, its windows in
neat rows across its face and with small, round towers
at each end of it. The walls were covered with creeper
and there were a lot of open windows, and one had the
instant impression that it was someone's well-loved
home.

They got out of the car and an earnest, elderly man
opened the door, to be followed at once by Prudence
and, more slowly, Haso.

Their welcome was very warm. Prudence kissed
Eustacia and then Colin, and Haso kissed her too before
shaking Colin's hand. 'Welcome to our home,' he said
and added, 'Eustacia, this is Wigge, who looks after us.'

She shook hands with him and went with Prudence
into the house. It was as charming inside as it was from
the outside. The hall was rather grand and the room they
entered was large and lofty and splendidly furnished,
but all the same it looked comfortably lived in—there
was knitting cast down on a table, newspapers thrown
carelessly down on the floor by a vast wing-chair and a
great many flowers in lovely vases. There was a dog too,
a Bouvier who lumbered to meet them and was introduced as Prince. Two very small kittens, asleep in an
old upturned fur hat, completed the reassuringly cosy
picture to Eustacia's eye.

'Come and see your room,' said Prudence presently.
'Lunch will be in half an hour, so there's time for a drink
first.'

She led the way upstairs and into a room at the end
of a corridor. 'Nice and quiet, it's at the back of the
house,' said Prudence. 'Here's the bathroom,' she
opened a door in the further wall, 'the dressing-room's
on the other side. I'll leave you to do whatever you want
to do, but don't be long.' She smiled and whisked herself
away, leaving Eustacia on her own to survey the room,

large and light and furnished with great comfort, with gleaming walnut and pale curtains and bedspread. The bathroom was perfection with piles of fluffy towels and bowls of soap and a white carpet underfoot, and from glass shelves there were trailing plants hanging. She paused just long enough to admire them and opened the other door. The dressing-room was a good deal smaller than the bedroom but well furnished, and Sir Colin's luggage was there. She went back to the bedroom, did her face and hair and went downstairs.

The rest of the day was taken up with an inspection of the house and garden, which was large and beautifully laid out, and in the evening there was a good deal of talk as to what they might do to amuse Eustacia.

'I don't need amusing,' she protested. 'It's lovely just being here...'

'It is nice, isn't it?' said Prudence happily. 'We'll go into Leeuwarden and spend some time shopping and the country around is worth looking at. Oh, and we must go to Sneek and Bolsward and Dokkum——'

'My love,' said Haso, 'they're only here for a week and Colin will be lecturing each day. I might even do some work myself...'

'Oh, well, I'll drive Eustacia round and perhaps we could go out one evening? There's Cremaillere in Groningen——'

'Or the Lauswolt in Beesterwaag——'

'We can dance there.'

Eustacia went to bed, convinced that no stone would be left unturned in the attempt to keep her amused during the next week. It was to be hoped that Colin would be amused too.

She saw little of him during the days which followed, although he returned in the late afternoon, when they would sit around over their drinks, talking over their day, and after dinner more often than not friends would call in, and on the second evening that they were there Prudence gave a dinner party for their closer friends and Haso's mother. Eustacia liked her at once, just as she liked his sister when Prudence took her to Groningen to meet her. Her days were full, but disappointment mounted as each day passed and Colin, kind and attentive as he usually was, made no attempt to be alone with her.

Her hopes rose when Haso announced that they would all go to Beesterwaag that evening for dinner and dancing. The hotel was some twenty miles away and they used Colin's car, the two girls sitting in the back, Prudence in russet taffeta and Eustacia in silk voile patterned in pink roses. The two men had complimented them upon their charming appearance when they had joined them in the hall, and Haso had given his wife a long, loving look which spoke volumes. Eustacia had had to be content with Colin's quiet 'charming, my dear', and when he had looked at her it was from under drooping lids which had allowed her to see nothing of his gaze.

The evening was a great success; they dined deliciously on lobster thermidor after a lavish hors-d'oeuvre, and finished their meal with fresh fruit salad and lashings of whipped cream, and since it was a party they drank champagne.

They danced too; Eustacia floated round with Colin, conscious that she looked her best. He was a good dancer and so was she, and she could have gone on forever. 'Enjoying yourself?' he asked her.

'Oh, so much, Colin. Only I wish you didn't have to be away all day.' To which he made no reply.

It was Haso, dancing with her later, who suggested that she might meet Colin for lunch in Groningen.

'Prudence can drive you there and you can come back with him later.'

He broached the subject later as they sat over their coffee, and Colin agreed placidly. 'Why not? The day after tomorrow, if you like, Eustacia, if Prudence doesn't mind driving you in.'

'A chance to do some last-minute shopping, since you'll be going the next day.'

It was when they were back home again and Prudence and Haso had gone into the garden with Prince that Eustacia found herself alone with Colin.

'You don't mind if I come to Groningen?' she asked.

'My dear girl, why should I mind?' he asked casually.

'You didn't suggest it yourself,' she told him angrily. 'We've been here for four days and you've never once wanted to——'

She paused, and he prompted, 'Wanted to what, Eustacia?'

'Be alone with me,' she muttered.

'True enough,' and at her sharp, angry breath, 'But I think that we must agree to Haso's suggestion, don't you? For the sake of appearances.'

She took a steadying breath. 'What have I done, Colin?' and then with a flash of rage, 'Oh, why did I ever come here with you, why did I ever marry you...?'

'As to that, my dear, we still have to have that talk, do we not? But somehow the right moment hasn't presented itself.'

'There is nothing to talk about,' said Eustacia icily, and when he put a hand on her arm, 'Let me go...' She darted away from him and up the staircase just as the others came back into the house.

Crying herself to sleep didn't improve her looks; Prudence took one glance at her slightly pink nose and said nothing, and after breakfast she suggested that they might drive over to Dokkum and have lunch there. 'The men won't be back until teatime and tomorrow you'll be in Groningen for most of the day.'

In the evening, when Haso and Colin came in, Eustacia was quite her usual self, rather more so than usual in fact. She wasn't a talkative girl usually, but this evening she excelled herself. When they parted for the night and Haso mentioned that she would be lunching with Colin the next day, she replied with every appearance of pleasure that she was simply delighted at the prospect.

'Well, you haven't seen much of each other,' said Prudence.

The men had gone by the time Eustacia and Prudence got down for breakfast. They ate unhurriedly and presently got into Prudence's car and drove to Groningen. Eustacia, listening to Prudence's chatter, was thinking hard. The time had come to tell him her real feelings. She felt quite brave about it at the moment, but probably by lunchtime her courage would have oozed out of her shoes.

They had coffee at Cremaillere before Prudence walked with Eustacia to one of the two central squares in the city. 'Go down there,' she advised, pointing to a crowded, narrow street, 'keep on for a few minutes and then turn to the right. Take the first turning on the left and the hospital's about five minutes' walk away. You are sure you want to walk? I could drive you there in no time at all...'

'I'd like to walk; it's my last chance to see the city and I've heaps of time.'

'Well, yes, you have—Colin's sure to be a bit late. You know what these lectures are—someone always wants to ask questions when he's finished. Have a nice lunch together.' She took Eustacia's parcels. 'I'll take these back with me—see you later.'

Eustacia started walking. It was really the first chance she had had of talking to Colin alone for any length of time, and she intended to take full advantage of it; there was such a lot she wanted to say and it was time it was said. She wondered if she could pluck up the courage to say that she loved him and ask what they could do about it, and as she walked she began composing various speeches on the subject. She would be cool and very matter-of-fact, she decided, and match his own bland calm. She was pleased with the speeches she was making up in her head, although it wasn't likely that he would reply as she imagined, which was a drawback. All the same, she had rehearsed what she would say, and was so engrossed that she didn't turn to the right but walked briskly over the crossroads and found herself in another busy main street. Another few minutes brought her to more main roads, and this time she remembered that she had to turn right—or had Prudence said left? She stood undecided on the pavement, and since she couldn't make up her mind which way to go she stopped a passer-by and asked.

'The hospital?' said the man in English. 'Cross over and take the left-hand road, walk for five minutes and then turn right. The hospital is in that street.'

He raised his hat politely and walked on and Eustacia, very relieved, did as he had bidden. She was already ten minutes late and she hurried now; it had taken her longer than she had expected but she consoled herself with the thought that Prudence had said that Colin would be late anyway.

The street was shabby, with run-down shops between small brick houses and here and there a warehouse, and the hospital loomed large halfway down it. She went through the swing-doors with a sigh of relief and approached the man sitting behind the reception desk in the gloomy hall.

She tried out her, *'Goeden morgen'* on his rather cross face and added, 'Sir Colin Crichton?' He stared at her without speaking so she added, 'Seminar, conference?'

He nodded then, said *'Straks,'* and, seeing that she didn't understand, pointed to the clock. 'Late,' he managed.

She smiled at him and asked, 'May I wait?' and took his silence for consent, and went and sat on a hard chair against the opposite wall. She was hungry and on edge and she hoped she wouldn't have to wait too long. It was half an hour before the lifts at the end of the hall began to disgorge a number of soberly clad gentlemen, none of whom bore the least resemblance to Colin. She watched the last one disappear into the street, waited for five minutes and then got up.

The man at the desk wasn't very helpful—he shook his head repeatedly at her attempts to make him understand until finally he picked up the telephone, dialled a number and handed her the phone. 'I speak English,' said a voice. 'You wish to enquire?'

'Sir Colin Crichton—I've been waiting for him. Is he still in the hospital?'

'There is no one of that name here. He was not at the meeting held here this morning. I am sorry.' The voice ended in a smart click as the receiver was put down.

There was nothing for it but to retrace her steps, and once she got to the square she had started from she would see if Prudence was still there; she had said she had more shopping to do and Eustacia knew where the car was.

She thanked the man and made for the door. It swung inwards as she reached it and she came to a halt against a massive chest.

'Where the hell have you been?' asked Sir Colin, and when she looked up into his face she saw that he was angry—more than angry, in a rage.

How nice it would be to be six years old again, she thought, then she could have burst into tears in the most natural way and even screamed a little...

'Here,' she said in a voice rendered wooden with suppressed feeling. 'Waiting for you.' She drew an indignant breath. 'You weren't here.'

'Of course I wasn't here, you silly little goose. You are at the wrong hospital. Although how you managed to go wrong when it was less then five minutes' walk from the square is something I fail to understand.'

'Understand?' said Eustacia pettishly. 'You don't understand anything—you're blind and wrapped up in your work and—and...'

'And?' prompted Colin, dangerously quiet.

'Oh, go away!' said Eustacia, and was instantly terrified that he might just do that.

But all he said was, 'The car's across the street. Come along.'

He shoved her into her seat with firm, gentle hands, got in beside her and drove off. 'Hungry?' he wanted to know.

'Not in the least,' said Eustacia haughtily.

'Good, in that case we might as well go back to Kollumwoude.'

And that was exactly what he did. And if he heard her insides rumbling he said nothing.

Prudence, standing at the window, saw the Rolls turn in and stop by the door. 'They're back,' she told Haso urgently. 'Something has gone wrong—just look at Eustacia's face, she can't wait to get into a dark hole and have a quiet weep. And just look at Colin...'

Haso came to stand beside her. 'Perhaps that's what they need—rather like a boil that needs to come to a head before it bursts.'

'Don't be revolting,' said Prudence and kissed him. 'What shall we do?'

'Why, nothing, my love. But we might have tea a little earlier than usual, as it is just possible that they've had no lunch.'

The blandness of Colin's face gave nothing away and Eustacia, never a talkative girl, gabbled her head off; the weather, Groningen and its delights, the splendour of its shops, the charm of the countryside all came in for an animated eulogy which continued non-stop until it was time for them to go to their rooms to change for dinner. Since it was the last evening of their brief visit there were friends and colleagues coming and Eustacia, quite exhausted with so much talking, came back from her shower and looked longingly at her bed, but the evening wouldn't last forever and she wouldn't need to talk to Colin; there would be enough guests to make that easy. She studied her two dresses and then decided on the black skirt and the top, which was a glamorous affair of cream satin exquisitely embroidered. She surveyed her person with some satisfaction when she was dressed, and went downstairs to find the men already in the drawing-room. Prudence followed her in, looking her magnificent best in a taffeta dress of hunter's green.

'That's nice,' she declared, studying Eustacia, 'and such a tiny waist.' She beamed at her. 'We're big girls, aren't we? And I'm going to get bigger...'

'I hope we shall be invited to be godparents,' said Colin.

'Well, of course you will. Haso wants a boy, I'd like twins...'

They drank a toast with a good deal of light-hearted talking and presently the first of the guests arrived.

It was after midnight when Eustacia got to bed; she had managed very well, hardly speaking to Colin during the evening but taking care that when she did she behaved like a newly married girl, very much in love with her husband. Which she was.

They left shortly after breakfast the next morning after a lingering goodbye to Prudence and Haso, and Eustacia, determined to preserve a nonchalant manner, made polite conversation all the way to Boulogne where they were to board a hovercraft. She hardly noticed that Colin answered her in monosyllables, she was so intent on keeping up a steady flow of chat. It did strike her just once or twice that when he spoke at all he sounded amused...

Their journey was uneventful, accomplished in great comfort and with a modicum of conversation. As they neared London Eustacia asked, 'Do you have to go to St Biddolph's tomorrow?'

'It depends. If you want to go to Turville you can take the Mini if I'm not free.'

She said, 'Very well, Colin,' in a meek voice; he sounded preoccupied, and if he didn't want to talk neither did she, she decided crossly.

Grimstone welcomed them with stately warmth, removed coats, luggage and Sir Colin's briefcase, ushered them into the pleasant warmth and a hectic greeting from Moses in the sitting-room and produced tea.

It was nice to be home, thought Eustacia, and was surprised to find that was how she regarded the house now. She poured tea and handed cake and Colin, with a word of apology, read the letters and messages with which Grimstone had greeted him. 'Nothing that can't be dealt with later,' he observed. 'Shall we phone Turville?'

The boys took it in turns to talk on the telephone, and then Mr Crump and Mrs Crichton detailed the week's happenings. Which all took some time, so that Eustacia had only a short time in which to tidy herself for dinner and have a drink with Colin, and even then there was no chance to talk even if she could have thought of something to say for Prudence rang up to see if they had arrived safely. Eustacia was glad of that for it gave her something to talk about while they sat at the beautifully appointed table, eating the delicious meal Rosie had cooked.

'Would you like coffee in the drawing-room?' she asked, conscious of the enquiring look Grimstone directed at her.

'Just as you like, my dear.' Colin sounded placidly uninterested, but he crossed the hall with her and sat down in his chair while she poured their coffee. They drank it in silence while she sought feverishly for something to talk about and, since her mind was blank, she poured more coffee.

'We have had very little time together,' said Sir Colin quietly, 'and, when we did, we have been at cross purposes. I think that it is time that we understood each other. Do you know why I married you, Eustacia?'

She put her cup and saucer down and looked at him thoughtfully. 'You wanted someone to look after the boys and love them and take care of them. Circumstances rather forced you into choosing me, didn't they? I don't suppose you had any intention of marrying me until it was—was thrust upon you...'

'But I had already asked you to come and live with us, had I not?'

She was a little bewildered. 'Well yes, as a kind of governess...'

'Would it surprise you if I told you that——' The telephone on the table at his elbow shrilled and he frowned as he picked it up. 'Crichton.' He spoke unhurriedly and listened patiently to whoever was at the other end. Presently he said, 'I'll be with you in ten minutes or so. No, no—not at all, you did right to call me.'

He got up and stood towering over her. 'I'm sorry, I have to go to the hospital. Fate, it seems, isn't going to allow me to tell you something I have wished to say for a long time.'

He was already at the door, but in the hall she caught up with him.

'What was it, Colin? Please tell me.'

He opened the door. 'Why not? I've been in love with you ever since I saw you that first time.'

He had gone. She stood at the open door watching the tail-lights of the Rolls disappear down the street until Grimstone, coming into the hall, saw her there and closed the door. He gave her a curious look as he did so. 'You feel all right, my lady?'

She gave him a bemused look. 'Oh, yes, thank you, Grimstone. Sir Colin has had to go to the hospital—I'm not sure how long he'll be.'

She went back to the drawing-room and sat down again with Moses and Madam Mop. 'Did you hear what he said?' she asked them in a whisper. 'That he was in love with me. But he never... I had no idea.' She drew an indignant breath. 'And fancy telling me like that just as he was going away.' The little cat got on to her lap and stared into her face. 'Yes, I know, he hadn't time to explain and I did ask him...'

She glanced at the clock—if it was just a case of examining a patient and giving advice he would be home soon. She put an arm round Moses, who had climbed up beside her, and fell into a daydream.

It was after eleven o'clock when Grimstone came into the room to tell her that he had locked up and ask, would she like him to wait up for Sir Colin?

'No, thank you, Grimstone, you go to bed. Rosie has left coffee on the Aga, I expect? I'll give Sir Colin a cup when he gets in.'

'As you wish, my lady. Shall I mend the fire?'

'No need. He won't be much longer and the room's warm. Goodnight, Grimstone.'

He gave her a grave goodnight, and went away. The house was quiet now save for the gentle ticking of the bracket clock and she sat, half asleep, waiting for the sound of the key in the door. The long-case clock in the hall chimed midnight and she got slowly to her feet. Surely Colin would be coming soon? He could have phoned, or was he regretting what he had said and deliberately staying away? She took the animals to the kitchen and settled them in their baskets and went back to the drawing-room. The fire was smouldering embers now and the room would soon be chilly. She put the fireguard before it, turned out the lights and went back into the hall, turned off all but one of the wall sconces and started up the stairs, to pause and then sit down on one of the lower treads, facing the door. If she went to bed she would only lie awake, listening for him . . .

The slow ticking of the clock was soothing, and after a few minutes she leaned her head against the banisters and closed her eyes.

It was half an hour later when Sir Colin let himself into his house. He stood for a moment, looking at Eustacia bundled untidily on the staircase, her head at an awkward angle, her lovely face tear-streaked, her softly curved mouth a little open. Being very much in love with her, he didn't notice the gentle snore. He closed the door, shot the bolts soundlessly, put his bag down and crossed the hall to stand looking down at her.

She woke then, stared up at him for a moment and then said, 'Would you say that again?' It wasn't what she might have said if she had been wide awake, but it was the first thought that entered her sleepy head.

He smiled slowly and the smile soothed away the tired lines of his face. He said very clearly, 'I have been in love with you ever since that first time—you wore a most unbecoming overall and I gave you a kidney dish. I didn't know it at the time, of course, I only knew that I wanted to see you again, and when we did meet I knew that I loved you, that you were part of me, my heartbeat, my very breath. It seemed that fate was to be kind to me when circumstances made it possible for us to marry, but then I began to doubt... You are so much younger than I, my darling, and somewhere in this world there must be a young man only waiting to meet you...'

Eustacia was wide awake now. 'Oh, pooh,' she said strongly. 'In the first place I don't much care for young men, and in the second place I love you too.' Quite unexpectedly two large tears rolled down her cheeks. 'I thought you didn't care tuppence for me, so I tried to be what I thought you wanted me to be.' She sniffed and he proffered a snowy handkerchief. 'We've never been alone...' she added dolefully.

'I didn't dare to be. But we are now.' He swooped down and plucked her to her feet and swept her into his arms. 'My dearest darling, we are now.' He kissed her in a slow and most satisfying manner, and then quite roughly so that she found it impossible to speak, and when she would have done, 'No, be quiet, dear heart, while I tell you how much I love you.'

'Oh, how very nice,' said Eustacia, managing to say it before he kissed her again. Then, 'I am so glad that we're married...'

She looked up into his face. His heavy lids had lifted and his blue eyes blazed down into hers. 'So am I,' he told her softly.

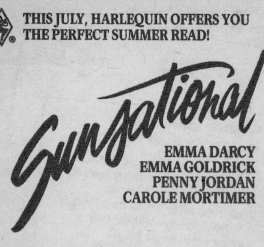

Coming soon
to an easy chair near you.

FIRST CLASS is Harlequin's armchair travel plan for the incurably romantic. You'll visit a different dreamy destination every month from January through December without ever packing a bag. No jet lag, no expensive air fares and *no* lost luggage. Just First Class Harlequin Romance reading, featuring exotic settings from Tasmania to Thailand, from Egypt to Australia, and more.

FIRST CLASS romantic excursions guaranteed! Start your world tour in January. Look for the special **FIRST CLASS** destination on selected Harlequin Romance titles—there's a new one every month.

NEXT DESTINATION:
FLORENCE, ITALY

 Harlequin Books

JTR7

Back by Popular Demand

Janet Dailey

Americana

A romantic tour of America through fifty favorite Harlequin Presents® novels, each set in a different state researched by Janet and her husband, Bill. A journey of a lifetime in one cherished collection.

In June, don't miss the sultry states featured in:

Title # 9 - FLORIDA
          Southern Nights
    #10 - GEORGIA
          Night of the Cotillion

Available wherever
Harlequin books are sold.